Nick grabbed her, and suddenly *she* was the one flat on her back. He covered her body with his. "Stop laughing," he growled.

"I'm…trying," she wheezed between giggles. The memory of his shocked look triggered another round of laughter.

Suddenly his mouth was on hers. The crazy man must have thought he could stop her laughter by kissing her.

He was right.

The feel of his lips molding hers stopped her midgiggle, and suddenly all she wanted to do was kiss him back. She poured every ounce of frustration, hunger, even anger into that kiss. She wanted him, desperately, had wanted him for so long. And even though she knew it was probably a mistake, that she'd hate herself for it later, she wrapped her arms around his neck and pulled him closer, letting him know in every way she could that she wanted this.

Undercover Twin

LENA DIAZ

First published in Great Britain 2013
by Mills & Boon, an imprint of Harlequin (UK) Limited.
Large Print edition 2013
Harlequin (UK) Limited,
Eton House, 18-24 Paradise Road,
Richmond, Surrey TW9 1SR

© Lena Diaz 2013

ISBN: 978 0 263 23825 9

Harlequin (UK) policy is to use papers that are natural, renewable and recyclable products and made from wood grown in sustainable forests. The logging and manufacturing process conform to the legal environmental regulations of the country of origin.

Printed and bound in Great Britain
by CPI Antony Rowe, Chippenham, Wiltshire

0556408

LENA DIAZ

was born in Kentucky and has also lived in California, Louisiana and Florida, where she now resides with her husband and two children. Before becoming a romance suspense author, she was a computer programmer. A former Romance Writers of America Golden Heart® finalist, she has won a prestigious Daphne du Maurier award for excellence in mystery and suspense. She loves to watch action movies, garden and hike in the beautiful Tennessee Smoky Mountains. To get the latest news about Lena, please visit her website, www.lenadiaz.com

Thank you,
Allison Lyons and Nalini Akolekar.

This book is dedicated to my parents, James and Letha McAlister. Daddy, you were a true hero. I thank God for every moment that I had with you. Mom, you have endured more heartache than anyone should ever have to endure. Your strength and grace amaze me. I love you both and am blessed to be your daughter.

Chapter One

Heather recoiled with disgust and turned away from the couple in the dark corner, their gyrating bodies moving as wildly as the couples filling the dance floor. Every beat of the music hammered at her skull. The smoky haze had her eyes watering. And the rancid odor of the sweaty mass of people seething around her had nausea coiling in her stomach.

Normally a seedy bar wouldn't faze her. She'd been in nearly every major nightclub in northeast Florida, let alone Saint Augustine, because of her job. The free-flowing alcohol lowered inhibitions and made gathering information far quicker and easier than an old-fashioned stake-out ever could. But tonight wasn't about work. Tonight wasn't about snapping pictures of a cheating husband in a compromising position for a couple hundred bucks. Tonight was about finding her sister, going home and soaking away her pounding headache in a tub full of strawberry bubble bath.

She clutched her purse to dissuade any greedy fingers from trying to pilfer her wallet and fought her way to the bar, like a salmon swimming upstream. By the time she found an empty stool to perch on, she'd been groped and propositioned so many times she was seriously considering exchanging her tub of strawberry bubble bath for a tub of hand sanitizer.

The bartender stopped in front of her. But even though his lips were moving, Heather couldn't make out what he was saying over the heavy-metal music pumping out of the speakers. He motioned to her and she leaned forward.

"What are you having?" he shouted.

She shook her head. "Not drinking. Looking for my sister, Lily. She looks like me. Have you seen her?"

"Do you have a picture?"

"I *am* the picture. She looks *exactly* like me. We're identical twins."

He wiped his greasy hair out of his face and squinted at her in the dim light. His mouth curved in a lecherous grin, as if he was considering the possibility of a threesome. "Sweet."

Heather's stomach rolled. She hopped off the bar stool, but the bartender waved for her to wait.

"Check the bathroom," he said. "I might have seen her heading in that direction a few minutes ago." He pointed to the dark hallway just past the couple who'd been enjoying each other so enthusiastically earlier. They both had silly, sleepy grins on their faces now. The guy looked at Heather and winked. She shivered with re-vulsion.

After thanking the bartender, she braced herself for another battle and fought her way through the throng of people to the pink neon sign that read Females and hung over the women's restroom.

When she pushed the door open, the strong smell of urine and stale beer hit her with gale force. She coughed and waved her hand in front of her face. If her sister wasn't in this bathroom, she was leaving. She'd go home until Nick was finished with whatever emergency his boss had called him about. And this time, when he offered to help her get her sister into an alcohol treatment program, she'd listen.

Just thinking about her new boyfriend of only eight weeks, his sexy half smile, the way his deep voice made her toes curl when he called her darlin', had her feeling better. It was wonderful having someone like Nick in her life. She was so tired of having to be strong all the time, with no one else to share her burdens.

"Lily?" she called out. "Are you in here?" She let the door close and stepped farther into the room. The lighting was even worse in here than out in the main part of the club, for which she was extremely grateful. She didn't want to know what disgusting substance was on the floor, crunching and sliding beneath her feet. "Lily?"

She made her way down the row of stalls, knocking and using the toe of her sneaker to nudge each door open. When she reached the last stall, she heard a noise, like someone taking a deep breath. "Lily, it's Heather. Is that you?"

"Don't come in here." The voice behind the last stall door sounded slurred, but there was no mistaking it.

Heather rolled her eyes. "Lily, are you drunk again? Is that why you called me to come get you?"

"I told you to come at midnight. You're early."
Another sniff.

She shook her head in exasperation. It was just like her sister to expect Heather to rescue her, but only on Lily's timetable, on Lily's terms.

"I have to get up early in the morning to meet with a new client. If you aren't ready to leave right now, and you're too drunk to drive, call a cab." She turned and headed for the door.

"Wait," Lily called out, her voice sounding mildly panicked. "Just give me a minute. My car won't start, and I don't have money for a cab."

Because she'd already blown all the money Heather had given her? Money Heather couldn't afford to give her in the first place?

Heather curled her fingers around her frayed purse strap and stepped back to the stall door. "What are you doing in there? Drinking? Haven't you had enough already?"

"Just wait at the bar. I'll be right out."

The airy quality of Lily's words wasn't lost

on Heather. Her sister sounded far worse than if she was just drunk. All kinds of scenarios flooded Heather's mind. None of them good. "Open the door."

Cursing sounded from inside the stall. "This is a bathroom. Give me some freaking privacy."

Heather hesitated. Arguing with her stubborn sister wouldn't do any good. It would just make her dig in deeper and fight harder.

"All right, I'll meet you at the bar." She walked to the door, her shoes crunching across the concrete. She stepped into the hall, turned around and tiptoed back inside, easing the door closed behind her. She quietly moved back to the row of stalls, pausing a few feet down from the stall her sister was in, so Lily wouldn't see her through the cracks around the door.

Loud noises sounded from outside the bathroom. Yelling. Feet shuffling. It sounded like people were running. What kind of craziness was going on out there on the dance floor?

Heather ignored the noise and waited. A moment later, the lock on the stall door slid back and Lily stepped out in her ragged jean cutoffs and tank top that showed far more than they concealed, including another new tattoo, a small pink dragon peeking out from the top of Lily's shorts. Her sister couldn't afford to buy her own groceries or gas money, but she could pay for a tattoo? Heather gritted her teeth. She was putting in eighty-hour workweeks—minimum— just to keep up with her car payments and rent. *She* certainly couldn't afford a tattoo, even if she'd wanted one.

She was about to give her sister another lecture on being frugal when she noticed what her sister was holding. In one hand she clutched a dark blue nylon backpack. In the other, she held a baggie of white powder and a rolled-up dollar bill. Heather's stomach sank. Now she knew why her sister was making those sniffing sounds earlier.

Cocaine.

Lily's eyes widened and her face went pale. Heather grabbed the baggie and ran into the stall. She tossed it in the toilet and pressed the handle.

"What are you doing?" her sister screamed. She dropped her backpack and shoved past Heather.

Heather stared in stunned amazement at her sister on her knees on the filthy floor, with her hands in an equally filthy toilet trying to fish out the baggie. Her heart breaking, Heather turned away, but a flash of white in Lily's backpack made her hesitate. She knelt down and pulled out a duct-taped brick of more white powder wrapped tightly in plastic.

Her hands started to shake. At least two more bricks of cocaine peeked out from the bottom of the pack. She couldn't even *begin* to imagine the street value of those drugs, or how many years in prison that would buy.

Lily looked back at her and cursed. "Give me that." She tried to get up, but her feet slid on the slippery floor.

Heather ran with the brick into the next stall and crouched in front of the toilet. She desperately ripped at the tape and plastic.

Lily stumbled in behind her, clawing at Heather's hair. "Stop, don't do it!"

Fire shot through Heather's scalp. She gritted her teeth against the pain and tore at the plastic, scooping the white powder into the toilet, flushing several times, using her body to block her sister until everything was gone but the tape and plastic.

Lily must have grabbed the backpack when she'd chased after Heather, because now she was cradling it against her, as if to keep Heather from taking the rest of her precious stash of drugs. She slowly slid to the floor, black mascara running in streaks down her face. "What have you done?" she moaned.

Sympathy and anger warred inside Heather as she stepped over her sister to get out of the stall. She was determined to leave her there, but she couldn't seem to make her feet move to the bathroom door. How many times had Lily dropped into her life over the years, staying just long enough to blow through Heather's totally inadequate savings account? How many times had Heather woken up to discover her sister gone again, moving on to the next sucker in her life, or her next big scam, or her next drinking binge—usually after stealing one of Heather's credit cards? How many times would Heather let her sister turn her life into a disaster and disappear until the next time Lily needed a place to crash?

Her shoulders slumped. She knew the answer to all of those questions. No matter how many times her twin hurt her, Heather would still love her, and she'd always be there for her.

She couldn't walk away and leave her sister, the only family she had, not like this.

She sighed heavily and turned around. "Come on. Let's go home. We'll figure out what to do, together."

"I don't want your help," Lily spat out. "I hate you. I always have."

Her sister's words shot like an arrow straight to Heather's heart. She drew a shaky breath, steeling herself against the pain. "Hate me all you want, but I'm still not going to leave you sitting on this filthy floor." She reached her hand out to help her sister to her feet.

Lily jerked back, like a wounded animal perched on the edge of a cliff, afraid to trust the one person who could save it.

A loud banging noise sounded behind Heather. She whirled around to see the bathroom door being held open as a group of six men dressed all in black rushed inside. Heather instinctively positioned herself in front of her sister.

"Federal officers, freeze!" one of the men yelled.

Federal officers? The man closest to her trained his gun on her while two others hurried down the row of stalls, slamming the doors open, looking in each one.

Heather stared in horror at the three white letters printed across their black flak jackets. *DEA*—Drug Enforcement Administration.

Her boyfriend, Nick, was a DEA agent.

One of the men grabbed Heather and pulled her away from the stall. Another one grabbed Lily and pulled her out into the middle of the room. Lily keened a high-pitched sound and fought to get away.

"Hey, be careful," Heather yelled. "You're scaring her." She tried to yank her arm away from the man holding her so she could help her sister.

"Let her go."

Heather froze at the sound of the familiar deep

voice behind her. The man holding her dropped his hands and stepped back. Heather turned around. The tall man filling the bathroom doorway, his short blond hair glinting in the dim light, was wearing the same dark clothes as the others and the same black flak jacket with the letters *DEA* across the middle.

Nick. Thank God. He'd know what to do, how to help Lily.

The look of shock on his face was quickly replaced with anger. His brows were drawn down and his jaw was so tight his lips went white. He looked mad enough to strangle her, but at least he wasn't pointing his gun at her, like the others. He held his gun down by his side, aimed at the floor.

He was probably furious that she was in the middle of this, and she couldn't blame him for that. She should have taken his advice. She should have tried to convince Lily to go into an alcohol treatment program. Then maybe Lily wouldn't have gotten mixed up with whatever she'd gotten herself into now. Heather had naively insisted she could help her sister on her own, without taking such a seemingly drastic step. But obviously Nick had been right.

Nick holstered his gun and strode toward her.

Heather was so relieved she almost slumped to the dirty floor. "Nick, I'm so glad you're here. Lily is scared. She's not—"

Nick roughly grabbed her arms and spun her around, shocking Heather into silence. He pulled her hands behind her back. She gasped at the feel of cold steel clamping around her wrists. A ratcheting sound echoed in the room, and he pushed her toward the door.

"What are you doing?" she cried out.

"Heather Bannon, you're under arrest." His voice was clipped, cold.

"What? Wait, what are you talking about?"

He paused beside the last sink and leaned

down, pressing his lips next to her ear. "You've got cocaine in your hair, darlin'," he growled.

Heather's gaze shot to the mirror. A wild-eyed woman stared back at her, a cloud of white dusting her normally dark brown hair, making it look prematurely gray.

Her horrified gaze met Nick's in the mirror. "I can explain."

"Tell it to the judge." He grabbed her arms and marched her out the door.

IN HER HIGH SCHOOL years, Heather had thought rock bottom was getting an A-minus on her trigonometry final exam, knocking her out of becoming the valedictorian.

In college, she'd thought rock bottom was flunking the GMAT and failing to get accepted into the master's degree program at Jacksonville University.

Later, when she'd been denied the small-business loan she'd wanted to start a private investigation firm, she'd thought that must surely be rock bottom.

But none of those were rock bottom.

Rock bottom was being arrested by her *former* boyfriend—there could be no doubt about that—and being thrown in a concrete-block holding cell that reeked of vomit and urine. A holding cell that currently housed five other women who looked like they could kill someone every morning before breakfast and never bat a false eyelash.

Heather didn't know where her sister was. The police had refused to answer any of Heather's questions about Lily. And no one had come back to update Heather or even give her the infamous phone call prisoners on TV shows always got. Not that she had anyone to call. Lily was her only family. Her friends had given up on her long ago when she'd started working seven days a week to try to build a P.I. business. And Nick... She shied away from that thought.

She was so tired. She wanted to rest her head against the wall behind her, but she was too afraid of lice, or something worse, that might be clinging to the surface. Instead, she stood a few feet away, trying not to touch anything, trying to pretend the speculative looks from the other women didn't send shivers up her spine. She was also trying her best not to give in to the urge to cry.

She was appalled that tears kept threatening to course down her cheeks. She couldn't remember the last time she'd cried, or the last time she'd even wanted to cry. She had Nick to thank for her jangled nerves. He'd judged her without giving her a chance to explain. He'd assumed the worst. Fine. Let him think what he wanted, but if there was any chance he was going to be the one to interrogate her—if anyone ever did bother to interrogate her—she wasn't going to let him see her with red eyes and tearstained cheeks.

She didn't want him to know how much his betrayal had hurt her.

A buzzing noise sounded and the door opened. A policewoman stood in the doorway and motioned for Heather to step out. "Miss Bannon, your lawyer is here."

"My lawyer? But I haven't even had a phone call."

The policewoman shrugged, her lack of interest stamped in her jaded, world-weary eyes. "Do you want to see your lawyer or not?"

Heather figured the police had made a mistake, that the lawyer was there for some other prisoner. But if playing along meant she'd get out of the foul-smelling cell for a few minutes, she wasn't going to argue. She stepped into the hallway.

The door buzzed closed behind her, and the policewoman led her down the hall to a door stamped with the words *Interview Room*. As she went inside, she braced herself, expecting to see Nick or a police officer waiting to grill her with questions. Instead, a stranger in a suit that looked like it must have cost at least a thousand dollars was sitting at a small table. He gave her a friendly smile and stood to shake her hand.

"Miss Bannon, I'm Anthony Greary, your attorney. A mutual friend hired me to help you out of this unfortunate situation."

The door closed behind Heather. She shook the attorney's hand and sat. "Mr. Greary, who is this 'mutual friend'?"

"Someone who prefers to remain anonymous."

The fine hairs on the back of Heather's neck stood at attention. "I don't suppose this friend is the man who gave my sister those bricks of cocaine?"

Greary glanced at the door and cleared his throat. "As I said, I'm here to help."

She had her answer. And it really sucked, because she'd *so* looked forward to a good half hour or more out of her cell. She pushed back her chair and stood. "I think you have me confused with my sister. My name is *Heather* Bannon. My sister is Lily. We're identical twins, but I assure you, we're nothing alike in any way that matters. And I guarantee we don't have any mutual friends."

"There's no confusion. I'm here to get both you and your sister released."

"Why?"

"Let's just say that one of you has something my employer wants returned."

Cold fear iced over Heather's insides. He had to be talking about the cocaine. What would happen if he found out she'd destroyed one of the bricks, and the police had the rest? Her hands started shaking. She clutched them together and gave the lawyer a false smile. "Like I said, there's been a mistake." She strode to the door and banged on the glass window.

A policeman Heather hadn't seen before

opened the door, a surprised look on his face. "You have fifteen more minutes, ma'am."

"There's been a mistake. This man isn't my lawyer," Heather said.

The cop looked past her into the room. He shrugged and led her back down the hall to the holding cell. At the door, he paused and pulled a key card from the pocket of his shirt.

"Wait," Heather said, desperation lending her voice a high-pitched tone. She *really* didn't want to go back into that cell. What if the other women had banded together while she was gone? What if they'd formed an alliance, like on those reality TV shows, and had decided to beat up the new girl just for fun, as a way to pass the time?

Panic was making her think crazy thoughts. But crazy or not, she couldn't help the tight feeling in her chest and the way her lungs were laboring to draw an even breath. She had to get out of here. Maybe she could talk to Nick for a few minutes and straighten this out. She hated to beg, especially when she'd rather punch him than look at him, but if she was here much longer they'd have to take her out in a straitjacket.

"Please, I need to talk to Nick Morgan and explain," she said. "He's one of the DEA agents who—"

"I know who he is, ma'am. But Special Agent Morgan isn't here. And he specifically said that if you asked for him, he didn't want to talk to you."

Heather closed her eyes, squeezing them tight against the ridiculous urge to cry again. *How could you, Nick? How could you judge me like this and throw away what we had, like I never even mattered to you?*

She opened her eyes and cleared her throat. "I believe I'm entitled to a phone call. I need to call a lawyer to arrange bail." Not that she could afford it. About the only thing she could offer as collateral was a four-year-old dinged-up

Ford Focus that had an outstanding loan balance higher than what the car was worth.

"I'll set that up," he said. "But you need to wait in the cell for now."

She managed not to whimper, barely. The policeman opened the door and impatiently motioned her forward. She steeled herself, took a deep breath and stepped inside. The odor of vomit hit her, making her eyes water, crushing the last remaining shred of affection she'd ever felt for Nick Morgan.

Chapter Two

Heather stood at the counter, rubbing her wrists, before taking the pen the policeman offered her. She could still feel the metal rubbing against her skin, even though the handcuffs had been removed. How long before she could forget that terrible night at the dance club, and being locked up for an entire weekend?

She scrawled her name across the form and handed it to the policeman in exchange for the belongings that had been taken from her when she was arrested. She deliberately checked her credit cards and cash in front of him. If the police didn't trust her and thought she was so dangerous that they had to lock her up, she wasn't going to trust them, either.

Satisfied nothing had been taken, she grabbed her keys. Wait. What good would that do? She plopped the keys back on the counter.

"Sir, officer, my car—"

"Is in the parking lot outside the station."

Relief had her smiling back at him in spite of her intentions. "Thank you." Darn it. She nearly bit her tongue. Why was she thanking him for moving her car from the club where she'd been falsely arrested? Bringing back her car was the least the police could do. Then again, it wasn't this police officer's fault. It was the DEA's fault.

One *particular* DEA agent's fault.

"Don't thank me," the officer replied. "Thank Special Agent Nick Morgan. He dropped your car off this morning, right after you arranged bail." He turned away to help someone else standing beside her.

Why would Nick bring her car back for

her? She certainly didn't think it was because
he cared about her. If he cared about her, he
wouldn't have arrested her. Or at the very least
he would have come to see her, maybe even
helped her arrange bail. As expected, the bail
bondsman had rejected her car as collateral.
She'd had to max out almost all of her credit
cards to get out of jail. Having already emp-
tied her savings to help Lily when she'd shown
up a few weeks ago, Heather now was down
to a paltry three hundred dollars in her checking account, and about five hundred dollars of
available credit on her last credit card. No, Nick
hadn't dropped her car off because he cared.
He'd dropped it off because it was his job.

She grabbed her keys and hurried toward the
exit. When she stepped outside, she was tempted
to drop to her knees and kiss the ground. But
she'd already suffered enough humiliation this
past weekend. She didn't want to add to it by
having someone see her on her hands and knees.

Instead, she settled for pausing long enough to take several deep breaths of fresh air, reveling in the pine scent from the nearby trees that was worlds different from the air in the holding cell.

Going home to a hot shower was at the top of her list of priorities. After that, she'd call the client she was originally supposed to meet Saturday morning and try to convince him, without telling him any details, that she'd had an emergency and still wanted his business. She couldn't afford to lose a client right now, not when her business was just beginning to make a profit and she had no more credit cards to fall back on to pay her bills.

Other than groveling to her client, she had no plans to work today, even though it was Monday. She hadn't taken a day off in nearly a year. And there was no way she could work right now. She needed some time to recover from her ordeal, and she needed to talk some sense into her sister. They also both needed to speak to the pro bono lawyer the court had appointed to defend Heather, and figure out what they were going to do about the drug charges.

The police had told Heather that Lily had been bailed out by the slimy lawyer who'd spoken to Heather about their "mutual friend." Heather would talk Lily into firing Greary. Lily would have to somehow pay the man back for the money he'd spent on her and use the pro bono lawyer Heather had been assigned. If Lily was going to survive this fiasco, owing money to a drug dealer's attorney was not the way to start.

When a couple stepped out of the police station, Heather moved away from the door and stood off to the side with her cell phone. She called her apartment three times, but Lily didn't pick up. Sighing, Heather shoved her phone back in her purse and shaded her eyes to look for her car. She spotted her gray Ford sitting in one of the spots right up front.

She headed to her car, but when she unlocked the door and pitched her purse into the passenger seat, she had the oddest feeling someone was watching her. She paused and looked around.

There, at the end of the parking lot, was Nick's massive black four-wheel-drive pickup. It was too far away for her to see details, but she could tell someone was inside. Was Nick watching her? Was he witnessing her humiliation as she left the police station in dirty, wrinkled clothes, her hair a mess, her makeup washed away long ago courtesy of a coarse rag and a filthy bar of soap she'd had to share with five other women? Was he waiting to see how broken she'd be after spending the weekend in jail?

She straightened her spine and got into her car with as much dignity as possible. It took every ounce of control she had not to slam the car door.

NICK TIGHTENED HIS hands on the steering wheel. The passenger door of his truck opened and his police detective brother climbed inside.

Rafe plopped down beside him. "Is that Heather, in the gray compact?"

"That's her."

"You could have come inside and talked to her. That would have been far less creepy than sitting here in the parking lot, like a stalker."

"She wouldn't want to see me."

"How do you know that?"

Nick scrubbed his face and blew out a deep breath. "Because I'm the one who arrested her."

"Yeah, there is that. But you also made me cash in my only chip with Judge Thompson to convince him to reduce her bail so she could get out of jail. Does she know you arranged that for her?"

"No." He glanced at his brother. "And she never will."

Rafe raised his hands. "I'm certainly not telling her, especially since you owe me, big time. You do realize I interrupted Thompson's weekly golf game?"

Nick winced. "What's that going to cost me?"

"Babysitting. For a month."

The dark cloud that had fallen over Nick since the night he'd arrested Heather lifted, if only a little, and he knew he was probably grinning like an idiot. Being an uncle to his oldest sister's two boys was one of the true pleasures in his life, especially since they loved football as much as he did. If Rafe's new wife was going to have a baby, Nick would gladly welcome another nephew into the family, or even a niece. Hopefully if the baby was a girl, she'd love sports, because the thought of having to sit through a tea party or playing with dolls had him breaking out in a cold sweat.

"Darby's pregnant?" he asked.

"Not yet, but we're working on it." Rafe grinned. "We're practicing. A lot. So I'm sure it won't be long."

"TMI, brother. *Way* too much information."

Rafe laughed but quickly sobered. "You didn't

call me out of a meeting to talk about my new bride. What's up?"

"Operation Key West."

"The task force that asked you to raid the club and promptly dumped you when Heather came under suspicion?"

"One and the same."

"I thought you were suspended. You can't be involved with a task force if you're suspended."

"Still suspended, pending an Internal Affairs investigation. But Waverly told me to come here to talk to the head of the task force."

"Here? Why would he want you to meet him at the police station? Why not meet you at the DEA office?"

"I asked the same thing, but Waverly just told me to get my butt over here for a ten o'clock meeting." He shrugged. "I was hoping you might have heard something. Captain Buresh didn't say anything about the DEA dropping by?"

"No, he didn't."

Nick stared through the windshield at the vacant spot where Heather's car had been a few minutes ago. Even now, several days later, he couldn't quite wrap his mind around the fact that Heather had been at that club the night of the raid.

"Maybe the head of the task force is here to discuss another local operation," Nick said. "Maybe Waverly wanted to make sure I met him before he left."

"Why would he want that?"

"Waverly's ticked at me. He might want to make me grovel and apologize for shaming our unit by having a drug-dealing girlfriend."

Rafe cocked his head and studied him. "From what you've told me about her, she doesn't sound the type to be dealing, just the opposite. She's been trying to build a private investigation business for years. She works all the time, putting everything she can into growing her client list. Do you really think she's going to risk throwing that away to deal drugs on the side? Her sister is—"

"Her identical twin."

"Okay. Not what I was going to say, but I'll go with that. Being a twin doesn't make two people the same and you know it."

"Yeah. Maybe. It did surprise me that she didn't let her sister's drug-dealer lawyer bail her out. If Heather had let him help her she could have been out of jail Saturday morning, like her sister. But she didn't, and she ended up staying in jail the entire weekend because of it." He shrugged. "I'm not sure what to make of that."

"You could always talk to her, give her a chance to tell her side."

Nick absently studied the rows of cars in front of the police station. Rafe was right. Heather did deserve a chance to explain. And he hadn't given her that chance. He'd been too angry, thinking she'd betrayed his trust in her. Now that he was thinking more clearly, he knew he'd made a mistake in judging her so quickly. But it didn't matter now. There was no way to fix this.

"I'm not allowed to talk to her now anyway, not with IA all over me. If I'm seen anywhere near her, I can kiss my career goodbye."

"You sure know how to pick 'em."

"What's that supposed to mean?"

"I'm just saying your judgment in women could use some work. You wasted nearly a year of your life with your on-again, off-again engagement to psycho-girlfriend."

"She wasn't a psycho. She was…conflicted."

Rafe let out a shout of laughter. "Conflicted? Now I know you've been talking to my therapist wife way too much."

Nick grinned. "Maybe. But psycho-girlfriend did have a lot going for her."

"Like what?"

"She was hot."

"Everyone you date is hot."

"She was a professional cheerleader. And very…limber."

Rafe smiled. "You've got me there. All I'm saying is that after everything you went through with her, I figured the next time you got serious about a woman you'd pick someone who—"

"Whoa, whoa, whoa. Who said we were serious? We only dated a couple of months. That's way short of serious territory."

"Darby and I only dated a couple of *weeks* before we got engaged."

"That's because her old-fashioned father knew you two had gotten 'friendly' and he shamed you into it. Besides, you two knew each other for years before you started dating."

Rafe rolled his eyes. "Her father had nothing to do with us getting married. And being on opposite sides in the courtroom doesn't count as a relationship. Look, all I'm saying is that you need to take a long hard look at your feelings for her before you do something you might regret."

"Meaning?"

"Meaning, if she didn't really matter to you, on a personal level, do you honestly think you would have twisted my arm to get the judge to reduce her bail? And how many DEA agents would have paid to get a car out of the impound lot and would have driven it to the police station for a woman they don't care about?"

Nick ground his teeth together. "I never told you about that."

"You didn't have to." Rafe gave him a smug look. "I have eyes and ears all over this town. That's part of what makes me a great detective."

"Humble, too."

Rafe shrugged, obviously not caring about Nick's insult. "As I was saying, you obviously care more about Heather than you're willing to admit, even to yourself."

"Since when did you become so touchy-feely?"

"I guess since I married a hot therapist."

"Whatever. I don't want to talk about this anymore. Not that I ever did."

"But—"

"Drop it."

Rafe held his hands up in a placating gesture. "All right, all right. I'll drop it. You said Waverly wants you to meet with the task force. You have to have some idea of why he'd want you to do that. And don't give me the line about apologizing for your girlfriend. That's weak."

Nick let out a deep sigh. Rafe always could read him, like a Jedi knight using the Force to probe his mind. Or was that Spock on *Star Trek?* Either way, it was damned aggravating.

"My DEA buddies tell me the task force still has Heather and her sister in its crosshairs," Nick said. "They think Heather's sister is running drugs for a dealer operating out of Key West. They think Heather's been helping her sister move the drugs, and that Heather flushed that kilo to try to avoid the sting. They believe she would have flushed all of the drugs if she'd had enough time."

His brother's eyes narrowed. "She couldn't have purposely tried to avoid the sting unless she knew about it ahead of time."

"Bingo."

Rafe swore. "That's the real reason they suspended you. Not because you're a terrible judge of character and got mixed up with a girlfriend who may or may not be dealing drugs. They think you tipped her off about the raid."

"If I were them, I'd probably think the same thing," Nick said. "I've been practically living in Key West this past year, building my cover to gather intelligence on the drug activity down there. Maybe they figured I've gone in a little too deep, that the past few months I spent up here were more than an extended vacation. Maybe they thought I was helping move drugs up the pipeline, and that Heather and Lily were in on it with me."

His brother cursed again, impressing Nick. With language like that, Rafe could go under-cover as a DEA agent and blend right in with the dealers as if he were one of them. Too bad he'd wasted his talents as a detective and part-time bomb-squad technician in the Saint Augustine Police Department.

"How can I help?" Rafe asked.

"Answer me a question. If you were heading up a task force whose sole goal was to catch a drug dealer with ties to Heather and Lily, what would you do right now?"

"If I was dumb enough to waste my talents as a DEA agent, you mean?"

Nick grinned. "Yeah. That's what I mean."

"If I believed the girls were a lead to a major drug dealer, I'd keep my distance. I'd wait for the dealer or some of his lackeys to show up." His gaze shot to Nick. "I'd use the girls as bait."

"Exactly."

Rafe groaned. "Ah, hell. You want me to keep an eye on your girlfriend for you."

"Ex-girlfriend. And I want more than that. I need you to keep her alive."

HEATHER FINISHED CLEANING the kitchen and stood with her hands braced on the edge of the sink. She stared through the cutout into the family room and shook her head. To say her apartment was a disaster was an understatement. Lily had always been incredibly messy, but this was the worst Heather had ever seen. Lily usually tried to confine her piles of dirty clothes and discarded items to her bedroom. This morning, Heather's entire apartment looked as if a tornado had gone through it.

Probably Lily's way of paying her back for flushing the cocaine.

Heather's shoulders slumped. She slogged her way through the mess to the short hallway that led to the two bedrooms. She paused outside the guest bedroom door and tried the knob. Still locked, like when Heather had first gotten home. She hadn't even seen Lily yet, because her sister was acting like a spoiled brat, hiding behind a locked door with classic rock blasting from the room. Heather banged her fist against the door. Still no answer.

"Come on, Lily. You can't ignore me forever. Open up. We need to talk."

Heather rested her forehead against the door. Maybe she should give up on her sister for now and get that shower she'd been longing for since she'd gotten home. The only reason she hadn't taken a shower already was because when she'd walked into her apartment the smell of rotting garbage coming from the kitchen had nearly knocked her over. How Lily could have ignored that smell was beyond her. It had permeated the entire apartment.

After taking out the garbage, Heather had started setting the rest of the kitchen to rights and one thing had led to another until she'd ended up scrubbing the entire room. Now the thought of a hot shower sounded like heaven. She might even soak her aching, tired muscles in that bubble bath she'd been wanting since Friday. She hurried into her bedroom, shut the door and took off her clothes.

NICK PAUSED IN the opening to the conference room, surprised to see an assistant district attorney sitting at the table, along with another man Nick had never met. His boss, Zack Waverly, was at the head of the table and motioned for Nick to come in.

Nick shut the door and took a seat beside his boss.

"Nick," Waverly said, "you already know ADA Tom Hicks. He only has an hour window before his next court appointment next door. That's why we met over here instead of at the DEA office."

Nick leaned over the table and shook Hicks's hand.

"And this," Waverly said, motioning to the man sitting at the other end of the table, "this is Special Agent Michael Rickloff. He works out of the Miami office and is heading up the Key West Task Force. He's the one who called and asked us to perform the sting on the club Friday night."

Nick shook Rickloff's hand. "Miami? You're not from Key West?"

"Miami native, born and raised. Key West is my current target, thus the name of the task force I put together. A major drug pipeline is coming up from the Keys into my city, and as you found out, even as far north as Saint Augustine. I want it stopped. And I need your help to do it."

Nick turned to Waverly. "My help? Is my suspension lifted?"

"Assuming you agree to Rickloff's plan, yes."

"But the internal investigation will continue," Hicks said. "And if we find anything that concerns us, you'll be pulled from the operation."

So that was why the ADA was here? To warn Nick to be a good boy? If it weren't for the carrot of having his suspension lifted, he would have gotten up right then and walked out.

Ignoring Hicks, he focused on Rickloff. "What plan? What operation?"

"When you raided the club for us, we were obviously hoping you'd find more than a knapsack with four kilos of cocaine. We were hoping you'd catch Lily Bannon meeting her contact here in north Florida. I wanted a bigger fish than Miss Bannon, to ultimately lead me to the head of the pipeline. Since that didn't happen, I need another way to bring my target down. That's where you come in."

Nick crossed his arms and sat back. "I'm listening."

AFTER PAMPERING HERSELF with a shower *and* a long soak in the tub, Heather was finally starting to feel normal again. She'd clipped her nails short the way she liked them and filed them smooth. She'd styled her hair into long curly waves that hung down her back, and she was wearing one of her favorite pairs of slacks—the soft, copper-colored chinos, with an exquisite pair of Italian leather sandals cushioning her feet—clothes she rarely got to wear because she was usually working.

Her typical work clothes consisted of T-shirts and jeans, things she didn't mind getting dirty or torn if she had to duck behind a Dumpster to avoid her mark catching her with her camera.

Thinking about work reminded her of the disastrous phone call with her client she'd made a few minutes ago—correction, *former* client. He'd been furious that she hadn't called him Saturday, and no amount of apologizing or telling him there was an emergency had soothed him.

Now she'd have to work extra hard to be even more frugal until she could get another big case lined up.

Determined not to think about her business and financial woes for now, she straightened the bathroom and went to work on her bedroom. Lily must have searched through all of Heather's drawers hoping to find some hidden money, because every single one of them was hanging open. Heather sighed and straightened the mess, then headed into the living room to tackle the mess in there.

She stood in indecision, not sure where to start. Not only were there piles of laundry, papers and DVDs lying around wherever Lily had chosen to drop them, but some of the drawers and doors in the entertainment center on the far wall were hanging open.

She blinked and studied the room more carefully. Was it a coincidence that her apartment was so horribly trashed, after everything that had happened? This wasn't a typical "Lily mess." It was far worse. The apartment looked like it had been…searched. She'd worried about Greary and his "employer" finding out about the fate of the drugs. Had they broken into her apartment and searched it? She gasped as an even worse thought occurred to her. What if Lily had been home when they broke in?

Her entire body started shaking. She whirled around and rushed back into the hall. She twisted the knob on Lily's door. Still locked. She pounded on the door, praying the awful, sinking feeling inside of her was because she was overtired and overreacting.

"Open up, Lily! Please. I need to know you're okay." She pounded on the door again. No answer. "Are…are you in there?"

Nothing except for the beat of the music, the same music that had been playing earlier, as if it was on a constant loop playing over and over.

Oh, no.

She ran to the kitchen, her gaze darting to every corner, as if someone might be hiding, ready to pounce on her. She yanked the junk drawer open beside the stove and grabbed the skeleton key before running back to her sister's room. She shoved the key in the lock and pushed the door open.

Shock had her frozen, pressing her hand against her throat. Everything in the room was shredded, as if someone had taken a razor-sharp knife and gone on a rampage. Nothing was spared. Not the drapes on the windows, the clothes in the closet that was standing wide open or even the comforter on top of the bed. Everything had been destroyed with a violence that sent a wave of fear crashing through her. And there, on the bed, was a small white piece of paper. A note.

When Heather read what it said, she whirled around and fled from the apartment.

Chapter Three

"You've been building an undercover presence in the Keys for quite some time," Rickloff said.

Nick shrugged. "About eight months, off and on, in preparation for a major op next year. We've been coordinating with the Key West office on that."

Rickloff waved his hand as though that was inconsequential. "That operation is a long ways off. My need is more immediate. I need you to use your cover now, on my task force."

"The Key West office is okay with this?"

Rickloff exchanged a glance with Waverly. "I haven't notified them yet, but I will. That's not for you to worry about. And I'm not asking much here. I just want you to help me draw out the big fish."

A gnawing suspicion started in Nick's mind, the suspicion that Rickloff wasn't being honest with him. Why would a task force out of Miami operate in the Keys without coordinating with the head of the Key West office?

"All right," Nick said. "I'll bite. Who's the big fish?"

"Jose Gonzalez."

"*The* Jose Gonzalez? The top of the food chain in the Keys?"

Rickloff nodded.

Nick snorted and shook his head. "Exactly how do you plan to get Gonzalez? The man has never even had a speeding ticket. Everyone knows he's dirty, that he's the biggest dealer around, but no one can ever get any evidence against him."

Rickloff leaned forward, his dark eyes blazing with excitement. "That's because they've never had the right bait. We've got his girlfriend up on charges that could put her in prison for years. If we make a deal with her in exchange for her cooperation, I think we'll be able to finally get enough evidence on Gonzalez to bring him down."

Nick had feared this would be Rickloff's angle. He'd expected it. But that was before he knew Gonzalez was involved. Using the girls as bait with someone like that was unthinkable, far too dangerous.

He looked at his boss, expecting him to speak up, but Waverly remained silent.

Nick cleared his throat and forced himself to speak in a reasonable tone of voice. "Let me get this straight. Are you saying Lily Bannon is Gonzalez's girlfriend? And that you want to somehow use her to bring Gonzalez down?"

"That's exactly what I'm saying. The two of them met about six months ago on a trip up here in north Florida. They've been a hot item ever since. Our CIs tell us Gonzalez actually thinks he's in love with Miss Bannon. We want to use that against him."

"Are these confidential informants people you've been working with for a long time? You trust them?"

"Absolutely."

"Then tell me how, exactly, you think you can use Gonzalez's affection for Lily Bannon against him?"

"Simple. We want you to be her contact in Key West. We'll make a deal with her. We'll drop the drug charges if she gathers incriminating evidence against Gonzalez and gives it to you. As soon as we have enough evidence to make a case against him, you'll pull Miss Bannon out. In return for *your* cooperation, we drop your suspension."

Nick turned to Waverly. "You do realize this is insane?"

Waverly turned a dull red. "It's risky, yes, but I think it could work."

Nick shook his head. "The problem here is that neither of you fully understand who you're dealing with. Gonzalez is a twisted psychopath. All the other dealers fear him. If anyone crosses him, in any way, he kills them. I don't care how much you think he may care about Lily Bannon. If he suspects for one second that she turned on him, that she's providing evidence to the DEA, she's dead. And exactly what makes you think you can trust an alcoholic and a junkie to hold herself together for this kind of operation? She'll crack under the pressure. And when she does, Gonzalez will pounce. There's only one outcome from this. Disaster. And I want no part of it."

He scooted his chair back from the table and stood. "I'd rather stay suspended than risk a woman's life. I'll take the paid vacation while Internal Affairs investigates me. And I assure you I'll be contacting Lily Bannon to advise her not to help you. It's far too dangerous."

Rickloff shot up from his chair. "You'll do no such thing. We need Miss Bannon's cooperation."

"Don't count on it." Nick strode to the door and yanked it open. He froze when he saw who was walking through the squad room toward him.

Rafe. And Heather.

Heather looked so pale the freckles on her face stood out in stark relief.

Nick met them halfway. "What happened? Are you okay, Heather?"

She shook her head but didn't say anything.

Rafe reached into his pocket and pulled out a clear evidence bag with a piece of paper inside. "Lily Bannon has been abducted."

THE CONFERENCE ROOM quickly filled with a mix of DEA agents and police officers. Captain

Buresh—Rafe's boss—barked out orders, along with Waverly and Rickloff.

Nick stared at the note through the plastic bag.

I've got what you want. You've got what I want. Let's trade.

The most obvious interpretation was that Gonzalez had abducted Lily and wanted to trade her for his kilos of cocaine.

So much for Rickloff's theory that Gonzalez was in love with Lily.

The second line of the note gave the location for the trade—Skeleton's Misery, a bar in Key West, along with tomorrow's date and the time of 9:00 p.m.

He glanced at his watch. It was eleven o'clock in the morning. That didn't give them much time to come up with a plan to save Lily. As soon as he'd seen the note, he'd run out to his truck to grab his map of the Keys. But when he'd returned, the conference room was in chaos. He'd tried several times to get everyone to be quiet, but no one was paying him any attention.

Rafe was leaning against the far wall, shaking his head, obviously as disgusted as Nick was.

Screw it. Lily didn't have time for this. And neither did Heather. She was sitting as still as a statue in her chair at the far end of the table, so ghostly pale she looked as if she might collapse at any moment.

Enough was enough. Nick raked his hand across the conference room table, sending folders, pads of paper and pens flying. The room went silent and everyone stared at him in shock.

"Now that I have your attention," Nick said, "I want everyone out except essential personnel." He plopped his rolled-up map onto the table. When nobody moved, he glanced at his brother. "Rafe, want to help me explain to everyone who the nonessential people are?"

Rafe grinned. Between him and Nick, they

went around the room directing people out the door.

Nick finally closed the door and turned around to a much more orderly, and quiet, conference room. The only remaining people were the same ones Nick had been talking to earlier, plus Heather, Rafe and Captain Buresh.

"You've got a bit of an ego to order all those people out, don't you, son?" Rickloff said.

"Lily Bannon's life is on the line. And we don't have a lot of time to figure out how we're going to save her."

He unrolled the map. Rafe grabbed some of the pads of paper off the floor and helped Nick weigh down the corners so the map would lie flat. Everyone except Heather gathered around the end of the table, leaning over the map while Nick drew a circle.

"That's Skeleton's Misery," he said, pointing to the circle on the western edge of Key West.

"It's a new bar that opened up this year. That's where Gonzalez wants to make the trade."

"Tell me about the location," Rickloff said.

Nick pointed to the street running out front. "It's one of the more isolated bars, at the end of the tourist strip. The street is narrow, more for walkers than cars. The nearest cross streets are a mile south, here—" he pointed to another spot on the map and marked an X "—and two miles north." He marked another X. "The only other access is from the ocean. There's a dock right behind it, again, fairly new. The bar caters more to locals than to tourists, so it won't be as crowded as some of the others, and there shouldn't be a lot of boats at the dock."

"What do you mean it caters to locals?" Waverly asked.

Nick glanced at Heather. Some of the color had returned to her face, and she was watching him intently.

"Heather, would you like some water or a bite

to eat?" Nick asked. "Rafe could take you outside, get you something."

Rafe was already heading to Heather's side when she raised her hand to stop him.

"I'm not going anywhere. I want to hear this. I want to know how you're going to help Lily." Her voice broke on the last word and she clasped her hands tightly on the table in front of her.

Nick belatedly wished he hadn't allowed Heather to stay in the conference room when he'd ushered everyone else out, but he didn't have time to argue with her.

"When I say the bar caters to locals," he continued, answering Waverly's question, "I mean it's raw. It's little more than a shanty with loud music. No fancy menus, no live bands, and the people who run the place are ex-cons."

Heather seemed to withdraw into herself and sank farther back in her chair. She was probably imagining her sister in that bar.

"I imagine the courts will insist on keeping

the kilos we got from the bar as evidence until the case against Lily and Heather is settled. So we'll need to check some kilos out of the evidence locker to use for the trade," Nick said to his boss. "Do we have that much on hand?"

Waverly shook his head. "I doubt it. Other than that bar raid, we haven't made a cocaine bust in quite some time. Any cocaine we've confiscated would have already been destroyed."

"*We've* got that much," Rickloff said. "Not a problem. I can have an agent bring the drugs down to the Keys and meet up with you."

"Good. We can place a couple of guys up the street here, and down here." Nick pointed to the map. "Gonzalez chose a good spot. There aren't a lot of hiding places. Maybe we could bring a few guys in from the water, have them hide out in a boat at the dock behind the bar."

"All right," Rickloff said.

"We'll have to pick an undercover agent who can pass for Heather in dim light." Nick glanced at Heather. "Five-two, small build, long, curly brown hair, blue eyes. Do you have any agents like that in your Miami office?"

Rickloff shook his head. "I don't have any women in my office."

Why did that not surprise him? Nick shook his head. He was less and less impressed with Rickloff the more he learned about him.

"I know the Keys office has some women, several of whom might be good candidates," Nick said.

Rickloff shook his head again. "I'm not ready to involve that office just yet."

Nick's suspicion that Rickloff might be trying to hide his operation from the Key West office had just been confirmed. But since neither his nor Rafe's boss were saying anything, he decided to let it go. For now.

"All right. There are five women in our unit here in Saint Augustine," Nick said. "But they're all taller than Heather." He glanced at Rafe. "Do you have any policewomen who could pass for Heather?"

Rafe shook his head. "I don't know anyone that small in stature here."

"There has to be someone we could use," Nick said. "We've got a state trooper headquarters down State Road 16. And the Saint Johns County Sheriff's Office isn't far from here. Or we could even ask for help from Jacksonville. Rafe, could you contact the other offices, see if they have someone available who fits the physical profile? The eye color may not matter. They could wear colored contacts."

Rafe nodded and pulled out his phone, but Rickloff shook his head.

"This is too important to risk using a look-alike when we've got an exact match for Heather Bannon sitting right in this room."

Nick swore under his breath. "You want to use Heather as bait."

"What I want, Special Agent Morgan," Rickloff snapped, "is to ensure that nothing goes wrong with this operation. We have a unique opportunity here. No matter what I've tried over the years, when it comes to Gonzalez, nothing sticks. I would have rather gone with my original plan to use Lily so I could get Gonzalez on drug charges. But they caught Capone for tax evasion. If I have to settle with getting Gonzalez for kidnapping, so be it. As long as I can put him away, that's what matters."

Nick stared at him in disbelief. "What matters is that we catch the bad guys without risking the lives of civilians. And please tell me you didn't just categorize a woman's abduction as a 'unique opportunity.'"

Rickloff's face flushed. "Poor choice of words."

"You think?" Nick crossed his arms. "You have the note. You have the time and location to make the trade. All you have to do is send in a team with an undercover policewoman and four kilos. If Gonzalez or his men show up, great.

You save Lily." He thumped his fist on the table. "And you don't risk the life of another innocent civilian by using her as bait."

Rickloff shook his head. "Gonzalez and his men know Lily too well. They'll expect her identical twin to look just like her. They won't fall for a stand-in."

"She'll keep to the shadows. Wear the same clothes, a wig. It will work," Nick insisted.

"If Gonzalez realizes we tried to trick him, he'll kill his hostage."

"You don't know that," Nick said.

"I'll do it." Heather's soft voice broke through the argument and everyone looked at her. She swallowed hard and fisted her hands on the table. "I'll be the bait. I don't want to risk my sister's life by using some other woman to pretend to be me. I'll do it."

Nick braced his hands on the table. "You are not getting anywhere near Gonzalez."

"Tom," Rickloff said, addressing the ADA.

"Are you willing to give Heather Bannon the same deal we were proposing for her sister earlier?"

Tom nodded. "We are. Her full cooperation in exchange for dropping the charges."

Heather glanced at Tom. "Drop the charges against my sister, too."

"Done."

"Then it's settled." Rickloff rubbed his hands back and forth. "Agent Morgan, you'll escort Miss Bannon into the bar. I'm not sending a civilian in there alone."

"Right, because you're so worried about her safety," Nick said, not bothering to hide his sarcasm.

"Nick," Waverly admonished. "You don't have anything to bargain with here. If you won't agree to this plan, we'll send a different agent to back up Miss Bannon."

"Really? Who? Who else could you send that has a built-in cover already? If you send someone without a solid cover, you risk Gonzalez thinking the DEA is involved. He'll kill Lily without even attempting an exchange."

Heather sucked in a breath.

Nick immediately regretted his candor. "I could be wrong." He didn't believe that, but he didn't want Heather to give up hope, either.

"Your concern for Heather Bannon's welfare is commendable," Rickloff said. "But you're over-thinking this. We'll have backup nearby. She won't be in any true danger."

Rafe made a sound of disgust.

His boss shot him an admonishing look.

"If Gonzalez pulls a gun on Heather," Nick asked, "can your backup get there faster than a bullet?"

Rickloff's jaw went rigid. "If you're convinced we can't protect her, then agree to the plan. You can be the one to protect her. You'll buy us the time we need to move in if something goes wrong."

Nick shook his head. "Find another way to save Lily and bring down Gonzalez. I'll take my chances with Internal Affairs. And Heather can take her chances with the judge."

He strode toward the door and yanked it open.

"Nick, wait," Heather called out.

He half turned, his hand still on the doorknob.

Heather appeared to be struggling for words. She folded her hands on the table and aimed her sad eyes at him like the sights on a rifle. "I can handle this. I'm an experienced private investigator. That might not seem like a big deal to a DEA agent, but it means I've been in a lot of tough, dangerous situations. I'm adaptable and a quick thinker if things don't go as planned. I'm also an excellent marksman, so I can defend myself, or watch your back. I *can* handle this."

"You're still a civilian, untrained in law-enforcement procedures," Nick said, softening his voice, trying to make her understand his concerns. "You shouldn't have to defend yourself against a drug dealer, or worry about watching anyone's back. You're also emotionally involved. That makes you vulnerable. And that makes you dangerous to yourself and everyone else."

Heather's eyes practically flashed sparks at him. "Look, I know Lily is screwed up, but she's still my sister. She's my twin. There's a bond between us other people—people without twins—can't possibly understand. It's like…we're two halves of a whole. If something happens to her, I don't…I don't know if I could survive." She drew herself up, lifting her chin defiantly. "I *am* going to do this, with or without you. But I'd feel safer if you were the one to help me." Her fingers curled into fists on the top of the table. "Nick, I'm begging you. Please. Help me save my sister."

The plea in her voice was difficult to ignore. But all he had to do was think about her being shot, or worse, tortured, by Gonzalez or his men, and his resolve hardened. He searched for the words that would make her accept the reality of the situation. "I've spent months, years, going undercover with guys like this. They live by their own code. They don't care about the law. If they even suspect you're lying, about anything, they'll try to kill you. Trust me on that."

"I do trust you. I trust you to protect me. I don't have to know much about the DEA to realize that these men wouldn't be arguing to get you to work on this case if you weren't the best agent for the job. I want the best for my sister. If you don't do this, Lily could die."

Her eyes were bright with unshed tears. It was probably killing her to ask for his help, after what she'd been through this weekend and his role in it. And watching her, listening to her, was tearing him up inside. But how much worse would it be if he gave in? No matter what angle he used to look at this plan of Rickloff's, he couldn't see any good coming out of it.

A tear slid down Heather's face and she wiped

it away, her face turning the dull red of embarrassment.

Nick swore beneath his breath and glared at Waverly and Rickloff. "You're both bastards."

Rickloff nodded. "Maybe I am. Maybe we both are. But when this is over, I have faith that Gonzalez will be behind bars."

"And do you also have faith that Lily and Heather will be alive? And unhurt?" Nick asked, his voice low and deadly.

Rickloff let out a deep sigh. "If you don't agree to help, I'm still sending Miss Bannon undercover with another agent. Is that what you want? For me to put her life in the hands of someone else? Someone who isn't as good as you? Someone who doesn't have as good a cover as you have?"

Nick swore again. He dropped his hand from the doorknob and turned fully around. He stared at Rickloff for a long moment before turning his gaze to Heather. Without looking away from her, he spoke to Rickloff. "All right. I'll go to Key West. I'll help you get Gonzalez and get Lily out of there. But I've got some conditions of my own."

Chapter Four

Waverly crossed the conference room to stand next to Rickloff. "Now listen here, Nick. You don't get to set conditions or make demands. You do what we tell you to do. You do your job." He jabbed his finger against Nick's chest.

Nick grabbed Waverly's wrist and held it in an iron grip. Waverly's eyes widened when he tried to pull his arm back but Nick didn't budge an inch. The look of alarm on his boss's face was almost comical. Waverly had only ever seen Nick in his "charm" mode. A smile, a joke, fast-talking, were Nick's usual methods for getting what he wanted. But when the situation demanded something more, he had no problem taking it up another level. Especially when a woman's life was at stake. And, as much as he hated to admit it, especially when that woman was Heather.

Only the fact that Waverly was his boss kept Nick from shoving his arm when he let go.

"I wasn't talking to *you* when I said I had conditions," Nick said. "I was talking to *her*."

Heather's eyes widened.

"Everyone out, except Miss Bannon," Nick ordered. He ignored Rickloff's and Waverly's grumblings as his brother and Buresh herded everyone out of the room.

Rafe pulled the door shut behind them, giving Nick a quick nod to let him know he'd guard the door.

Nick stood directly in front of Heather's chair and leaned down, intentionally using his size to try to intimidate her. "You aren't going to Key West," he growled. "With *anyone*."

She raised her chin defiantly and crossed her arms over her chest. "Yes. I am."

"No. You aren't. You're going to stay here. You're going to move in with my brother for a few weeks. He's a police officer, a damn good one. He'll keep you safe in case Gonzalez's buddies come looking for you. I'll go to Key West and try to get your sister out of this mess. But no way in hell are you coming with me."

She was shaking her head before he finished his last sentence. "No. You heard Rickloff. He said Gonzalez will kill Lily if I'm not in that bar to meet him. I am going. With or without you."

"I've been on dozens of undercover operations. What Rickloff is asking you to do sounds too simple, too easy. Nothing in the world of drug dealers is that simple or easy. He's hiding something."

"Like what? Why would he hide anything?"

"I don't know. But it doesn't feel right. It doesn't pass the smell test. I don't trust Rickloff.

He's from the Miami office, leading a task force to capture a dealer in Key West. But he hasn't notified the special agent in charge at the Key West DEA office. Something isn't right here. Rickloff's motives are suspect, and this plan of his is far too dangerous and risky."

"Okay, what's the alternative? How do we find my sister and get her back safely?"

He shoved a hand through his hair and blew out an exasperated breath. "I haven't figured that out yet."

"Well, we don't have time for you to figure it out."

Nick stared down at Heather, surprised at how stubborn she was being. She'd always been so easy to get along with. She could be the hard-nosed P.I. when she had to be, but he'd seen the soft, passionate, feminine side of her and had never expected her to defy him like this.

The only time they'd ever argued was after a phone call between Heather and her sister.

When Heather told Nick her frustrations about Lily's behavior, he'd flat out told her Lily was a drunk and needed to be in treatment. Maybe he could have worded his conclusions in softer language, but when Heather had insisted her sister wasn't an alcoholic, the two of them had ended up in a heated discussion.

She hadn't backed down one bit and he'd ended up apologizing, even though he firmly believed she was wrong. Now, as he stood in her personal space, purposely trying to intimidate her into giving in, he wasn't having any more luck than he'd had the first time they'd argued. Instead, she stared up at him, her eyes flashing with anger. And something else.

Fear.

She *should* be afraid, for *herself.* But he knew she wasn't. She was afraid on behalf of her sister, and recklessly willing to do anything to help her, even if it meant putting herself in danger. He finally accepted that no amount of arguing was going to change her mind. Intimidation wasn't going to work. He sighed.

"I'll help you get Lily back," he said, "but like I said earlier, I have conditions."

She darted her eyes toward the closed door, as if by sheer will she could get Waverly and Rickloff to step inside. "What conditions?"

"First, we're through, finished. There is no 'us' anymore. And there never will be."

"Agreed."

She answered so quickly Nick was taken aback. He'd been prepared to explain about his job, how he couldn't date anyone tainted by illegal drug activity, even indirectly through a family member. He'd planned to tell her he still cared about her, that he regretted how things had turned out. But there was no point in apologizing now, not when *she* so obviously didn't want a relationship with *him* anymore.

That knowledge stung far more than he would have expected.

He rested his hip against the table. "Second, you do exactly what I tell you to do at all times. I mean it. Exactly what I say. Unquestioningly. If I tell you to get down, you drop on the floor as if someone had swiped your legs out from beneath you. If I tell you to be quiet, you don't even breathe until I tell you it's safe. Can you do that?"

Her eyes widened with alarm, as if she was just beginning to realize how dangerous this mission was.

"O-okay," she said, her voice soft, hesitant.

"Three, you report to me and me alone. I don't care what Rickloff or Waverly tell you. One phone call to them at the wrong place, wrong time, could get us killed—you, Lily and me."

"Why would you think they would ask me to call them?"

"It's what I'd do if I were them."

She nodded. "Okay. Is that all?"

He shook his head. "No, there's one more

condition. And it's a deal breaker. You already agreed to my other conditions. Remember that. One of those conditions was to do exactly what I tell you to do."

"I understand."

"Okay. Final condition. We'll go to Key West together, but you'll stay in hiding, in my hotel room with another agent watching over you, while I go to that bar to draw Gonzalez out somehow. I *will* figure out a way to save your sister, but I refuse to use you as bait. It's too dangerous."

She raised her hands in a gesture of surprise and frustration. "How will we save Lily if I'm in hiding?"

"Leave that to me. You have my word I'll do everything I can to save her, but putting you in danger is not part of the plan. I meant what I said. This is the deal breaker. You agree to this or I'm out. And you already know I'm the best agent for the job or Rickloff wouldn't have tried so hard to convince me to do this. So what's it going to be?"

She stared at him for a full minute, frustration and anger warring with each other across her expressive face. Even though she didn't want to agree to his final condition, she obviously knew he was her sister's best shot at making it out of Key West alive.

He glanced at his watch, well aware of how urgent it was to get moving soon or there wouldn't be a chance to help Lily at all.

Heather let out a long breath and glared at him, obviously not happy, but resolved.

"I guess I don't really have a choice," she said. She shoved out of her chair and headed to the door.

"You made the right decision," Nick said.

"I hope so." She paused in the door opening. "Because I've decided Lily's best chance is with someone *other than you.*"

NICK AND RAFE leaned back against the desk in the SAPD squad room. They both had their legs spread, arms crossed, as if they had nothing better to do than to watch the fiasco playing out in front of them.

Waverly and Rickloff stood on the other side of the room with the small group of agents who'd come up from Miami with Rickloff, talking to Heather. Apparently they were giving her last-minute instructions while one of the agents grabbed her suitcase that she'd gone home and packed after telling Nick she didn't want his help. Her refusal to trust him still stung, but he supposed he'd earned that by letting her sit in jail all weekend and not giving her a chance to explain what had happened.

"I heard they're flying out to Key West in the morning," Rafe said. "They're going to a hotel by Jacksonville International Airport for tonight."

Nick grunted in reply.

"They'll arrive at the Key West airport around noon," Rafe said. "An agent from Miami will meet them there with the kilos and drive Heather to a hotel. I might have even heard a rumor about which hotel they'll be using."

"One of those infamous contacts you brag about, I suppose?"

"Yep."

"I don't suppose you also know the name of the Miami agent they've chosen to go to the bar with Heather?"

"I might."

"That could prove useful."

They watched in silence as Heather shook Rickloff's hand. She and the entire entourage headed across the far side of the squad room toward the exit. Heather didn't even look Nick's way.

"Are you sure you've made the right decision?" Rafe asked, stifling a yawn as he, too, watched the group head to the exit.

"Yep."

"If Waverly fires you, I could put in a good word for you at SAPD," Rafe said. "We have an opening for a meter reader. A washed-up DEA agent might be qualified for that."

Nick shoved him.

Rafe shoved him back.

Waverly held the door open for Heather, and the small group headed out front. They stood at the curb, apparently waiting for the van from the airport that was heading toward the front of the building from the end of the parking lot.

"He's not going to fire me," Nick said.

"You sure about that? He seemed pretty ticked that you didn't go along with Rickloff's plan. I haven't seen his face that red since you cleaned him out at poker a few months ago."

Nick sighed. "I miss poker nights. I can't believe you let Darby cancel our poker nights."

"Let her? Are you implying the decision

wasn't mine? That she has me wrapped around her finger?"

"I'm not *implying* anything. You're her lap-dog. Ruff, ruff."

"I'll pay you back for that."

"Looking forward to it."

"This is serious. You could lose everything."

"Yeah. I know," Nick said quietly. "But I'm still going through with it."

While Heather's luggage was being loaded, she and her entourage got inside the van. Apparently they were all accompanying her to the airport hotel. Nick supposed that was their way of pretending they were actually protecting her instead of sending her into an impossible situation where the odds of her being hurt, or killed, were enormously high.

The van slowly took off, as if it had all the time in the world.

Nick tapped his hand on the top of the desk beside him as he and Rafe watched the van's slow progression. The van turned the corner and disappeared.

"Where is it?" Nick demanded, shoving away from the desk. He grabbed his go-bag of clothes and toiletries from where he'd hidden it inside a small office trash can.

Rafe reached behind him and grabbed a set of keys from out of a folder. "First row." He tossed the keys to Nick, who was already running toward the exit. Nick caught them midair and ran outside. He heard Rafe running to catch him, but he didn't wait.

He sprinted around the corner of the building.

"Damn it, Nick. Hold up."

Nick stopped at the narrow chain-link gate, but only because he didn't have a key to open it. "Hurry," he said, as Rafe pulled his key card from his pocket. "It's a long drive and I've got a lot to do before they get there tomorrow."

"I'm hurrying, I'm hurrying." The gate buzzed and Rafe pulled it open.

Nick ran inside, immediately spotting the car Rafe was letting him borrow from the impound lot. He whistled and ran his hands lovingly over the sleek contours of the red Maserati Gran-Turismo convertible.

Rafe caught up to him and called him a name that would have given their mother a heart attack, especially coming from her oldest, the son who could do no wrong.

Nick grinned. "You're jealous I get to drive this sweet baby."

"No. I think you're a fool to have chosen this car out of all the ones I told you about. I would have chosen the black Lamborghini over there in the corner. Much less flashy."

"Flashy is the point. It's what my low-life friends expect down in the Keys. Besides—" he opened the door, pitched his go-bag onto the passenger floorboard and paused "—I may need a backseat. You never know when you'll have to carry something, or someone, and need the room."

Rafe exchanged a long glance with him, obviously understanding Nick's meaning. If Heather and her Miami agent ran into trouble, Nick might end up being their only way out. He couldn't do that with a two-seater.

"Don't scratch it," Rafe said as he closed the door. "And no bullet holes this time. There was hell to pay the last time I let you borrow a car. I mean it. Not even a scratch." He ran to the car gate a few feet away and pressed the button that started the gate sliding back on its rails.

Nick started the engine and backed out of the parking space. He would have preferred to get a car from the DEA impound lot, but his boss knew him too well. He'd given express orders that Nick wasn't allowed to check out any vehicles.

As soon as the gate was open wide enough for him to squeeze through, he stomped the accelerator. The car jumped forward like a gazelle, swift and graceful. He waved at Rafe as he zoomed by. He had to ease his foot off the gas to maneuver through the narrow, winding road by the police station. But as soon as he reached US 1, he turned the car south and let the horses run.

Normally when he got to drive one of the impounded sports cars, he would marvel at the perfectly tuned engine or the luxurious feel of Italian leather seats he'd never be able to afford in an entire lifetime of working for the DEA.

But not today. Today he was more concerned with the clock in the dashboard.

He had less than thirty-two hours to figure out how to save Lily and Heather without getting himself or anyone else killed.

Chapter Five

Heather had assumed Nick was exaggerating when he'd described the rough atmosphere of the Key West bar called Skeleton's Misery. But it was just as seedy as he'd said it would be. Still, it's not like she was alone, defenseless. Mark Watkins, the undercover DEA agent assigned to work with her, was sitting beside her. And Rickloff had backup outside somewhere, ready to come to the rescue at the slightest hint of trouble. But even with Mark and backup nearby, a shiver of apprehension still lanced down Heather's spine—because this was definitely *not* a typical bar, and Nick had definitely *not* exaggerated.

She avoided eye contact with the men around them, men who looked like Satan's personal biker gang, draped in black leather and silver chains, and covered with tattoos of snakes, dragons and naked women. She'd glimpsed knives peeking out from beneath some of their jackets. Big knives that made the pocketknife she usually carried around for emergencies—the one she'd had to ditch to board the airplane—look like a harmless toy. And she was fairly certain she'd glimpsed guns beneath some of their jackets, too.

Everyone in the bar seemed to be taking turns staring at her and Mark with open hostility and suspicion while the two of them sat at one of the high-top tables, sipping their beers. She was the only woman in the bar. And from what she could tell, she and Mark were the only "nonregulars." It was as if they'd intruded into someone's home without an invitation, or into a drug dealer's lair where his minions were planning their next big score.

Mark pretended to be absorbed in the football game on one of the TVs suspended from the ceiling. At least, Heather hoped he was pretending.

A large duffel bag sat at their feet, with four bricks of cocaine concealed inside. She didn't want to think about what might happen to her and Mark if Satan's bikers realized what was in that bag. She imagined there would be a violent frenzy, like a group of man-eating sharks scenting blood in the water.

"It's nine-fifteen, Mark," she whispered. "Shouldn't he be here by now?"

"Don't use my real name." Mark's reminder was said in a quiet voice Heather had to strain to hear over the loud TVs and music.

"Look, honey." He pointed to the football game and spoke louder as if for the benefit of those around them. "We're in the red zone. We might pull this one out after all."

Heather rolled her eyes. It was Tuesday night. She and every football fan in America knew that any football game on tonight was either a highlight reel or a replay of an old game. The TV above the bar was tuned to ESPN Classic, which was replaying a Tampa Bay Bucs game Heather had seen firsthand last season in Raymond James Stadium. She'd heard the cannons boom to celebrate the score that clinched the game. Obviously Mark wasn't a football fan or he'd have known that. Her respect for him plummeted and she shook her head.

Another half hour passed. Angry mutterings started around them. The bartender gave her and Mark pointed looks as if to warn them their presence wouldn't be tolerated much longer.

Heather risked another glance around the room. She didn't know what Gonzalez looked like, but *he* knew what *she* looked like. If he was in the crowd, surely he'd have spotted her by now and would have approached her table. The note he'd left at her apartment had been clear about the time—nine o'clock. Well, nine o'clock had come and gone over forty-five minutes ago. What did it mean that no one had shown up to make the trade? What did that mean for Lily?

She jumped at the feel of a hand on top of hers.

Mark was leaning over, his mouth next to her ear. "I don't like the looks of the guys who just came in. Let's get out of here."

He didn't like *their* looks? Was it possible for someone to be scarier-looking than the men already in this place? Heather started to turn, but Mark put his arm around her shoulder.

"Don't look at them. Let's go." He pitched some tip money on the table and stood.

Heather clutched the edge of her bar stool. "But we can't leave. Lily—"

"We'll figure it out later. We've got to go. Now. Trust me."

Trust me. The last person who'd told her that was Nick. Had she been wrong not to trust him? Had she made a mistake that had just cost her sister her life?

She took a deep breath, trying to stave off the panic that was threatening to consume her.

Mark tugged the strap for the duffel bag over his shoulder and grabbed her hand, hauling her toward the door.

The moment they were outside, reality slammed into Heather like a physical thing, twisting inside her chest, threatening to make her double over and freeze like a terrified rabbit. She had to lock her emotions away. She couldn't give up yet. There was still a chance she could save Lily. *There had to be.*

Mark pressed his hand at the small of her back, urging her to move.

"There are four of them," he whispered a minute later. "And they're definitely following us."

"What about our backup?"

"They should be here any second. I said the code word into my transmitter. They know we need help. That's why we went outside, so Rickloff's men can grab the guys behind us without having to fight every man in that bar. We'll be fine."

Since his fingers were currently digging painfully into her back as he propelled her along, she wasn't so sure that *he* believed everything was fine.

He led her down the sidewalk back toward their motel, which was little more than a collection of cottages a block off the water, with a pool out back and a stage where live bands played every night. Although the sun had set hours ago, the moon was full and bright, guiding their way.

The knot in Heather's shoulders began to ease

when the sign for their motel came into view. It wasn't far now, four, maybe five blocks. Unfortunately, the businesses in this section were dark and closed up for the night. Apparently the tourists didn't venture this far down except in the daytime. What had Rickloff been thinking to put them in such an isolated area? Had he realized what he was doing when he'd chosen their motel?

Again Nick's warnings flitted through her mind. He'd seemed unimpressed when he realized Rickloff was from Miami. Was this why? Did he fear that Rickloff would make mistakes because he wasn't familiar enough with the Keys? That sounded like a no-brainer to her, but she'd assumed Rickloff would have had good intel on the area. Looks like she'd put her faith in the wrong people after all. Once she got back to the motel she was going to demand to speak to Rickloff.

"Cross to the other side," Mark's urgent whisper sounded in her ear.

He grabbed her hand and pulled her across the street to the other sidewalk.

"Don't look back," he whispered. "Keep walking."

The worry in his voice sent a sinking feeling through her stomach. He wasn't even trying to pretend anymore that he wasn't concerned.

He suddenly smiled and leaned down as if to say something suggestive in her ear, and casually glanced over his shoulder. He uttered a foul curse.

"Rickloff," he growled into the parrot pin transmitter attached to his shirt, "get some backup over here, now."

He'd called Rickloff by name, something he'd repeatedly warned *her* not to do. And he hadn't used any code words.

They were in deep trouble.

Heather bitterly wished the DEA had allowed

her to bring her own gun. She didn't like having to rely on someone else to protect her. And Mark was hopelessly outnumbered if the men behind them all had guns.

Three blocks to go. The registration booth for the motel was dark and deserted, but the lazy tune of "Margaritaville" piped out into the night from the live stage behind the collection of cottages.

Footsteps sounded behind them. So close!

They weren't going to make it to the motel.

"What are we going to do?" she cried out.

Mark's gaze darted to the left and right of the street, as if he was still expecting someone to come to their aid. But the backup Rickloff had promised at the first hint of trouble was nowhere to be seen.

"Mark?" Heather tried not to let her panic show, but his name still came out as a high-pitched squeak.

"When I say go," he said, "I want you to make

a run for the motel. Run straight to the back by the pool where all the people should be, right up on the stage with the band if you have to. Tell someone to call the police. You got that?"

"But what about you? What are you going to do?"

"Stall them. Go, Heather, run!" He shoved her forward, dropped the duffel bag and whirled around to face their pursuers.

Heather took off running. Shouts sounded behind her. She didn't dare look back. She pumped her legs as fast as she could, whimpering when she heard the sound of a single pair of footsteps pounding behind her, getting closer and closer every second.

A shot rang out.

She let out a startled yelp. Was that Mark's gun or someone else's?

Tires squealed. Headlights flashed. A car barreled up the street in her direction. She hesitated. The motel was still too far away. She turned around. A man was charging toward her. She screamed and sprinted to the car, praying the driver wasn't working for Gonzalez, and that he wasn't friends with the man trying to catch her.

Brakes screeched. The sleek red convertible with its top down rocked to a halt beside her.

"Get in."

Heather gasped at the sound of that deep, familiar voice.

Nick Morgan.

He wasn't looking at her. He was holding a gun and appeared to be aiming it at the man behind her. Heather jumped over the passenger door and plopped down onto the seat. She glanced back in time to see the man who was chasing her dive into some bushes on the side of the road.

Nick shoved his gun in the middle console and hit the accelerator. The car leaped forward.

Heather grabbed the armrest to keep from

sliding across the leather seat. "There was an agent with me. He's over—"

"I know. Get down."

Remembering condition number two, she immediately turned around and slid off the seat onto the floorboard, or at least as much as she could, folding herself into the tiny space between the dashboard and the seat.

Nick grinned, apparently thinking it was amusing to see her slide down onto the floor. The crazy man was actually having fun.

The car lurched and skidded sideways. Someone lunged over the top of the door on Heather's side of the car and fell into the backseat. Heather had just enough time to realize it was Mark before Nick punched the accelerator again. Someone shouted from a few feet away. Another man cursed. The deep boom of a powerful gun filled the air. Heather jerked in surprise. The crunch and crackle of safety glass told her the shot had punched a hole in the windshield, but the rest of the glass held together.

Nick grabbed his gun, shaking his head and mumbling something about how Rafe was going to kill him. He fired two quick shots and shoved his gun into the console again. The tires screeched as he wheeled the car around in the middle of the narrow street, facing back in the direction he'd come from. The engine roared and the car rocketed forward, flying down the two-lane road into the night.

Heather couldn't move. She was too stunned by what had happened, frozen in place. She stayed curled up, half on the seat and half on the floor, clutching the armrest and console to keep from sliding around.

Nick continued his reckless pace, twisting and turning down side roads. The few houses they passed dropped away until there was nothing but dark trees whipping by.

Mark pulled himself into a sitting position,

hooking an arm around the back of the passenger seat in front of him to brace himself, but still no one said anything, as if they were all too shell-shocked from what had just happened, or in Nick's case, too focused on getting away.

Heather caught glimpses of the ocean sparkling in the moonlight through the groves of trees on the side of the road. Nick finally slowed down and turned the car. Heather risked a quick peek and saw he was driving them up a long, sloping driveway. He pressed a button on the sun visor. Moments later he pulled into a garage and pressed the button again. The garage door slowly lowered, cocooning them inside.

After Nick cut the engine, for the space of several heartbeats, no one moved. Nick stared straight ahead as if deep in thought. Finally, he looked down at Heather. "Are you all right?"

She nodded, slowly unfolding herself from her painfully tight position. She turned around and plopped down on the seat. "Why are you here? How did you know we needed help? Where are we?"

He scrubbed his face and rolled his shoulders as if to relieve some stiffness. "You're welcome," he said, his voice sounding bland.

Heather's face flushed hot as she realized how ungrateful she must have sounded. "Thank you. I mean it. Really, thank you, thank you, thank you. You saved our lives back there."

The corner of his mouth quirked up with amusement. "One thank-you would have been sufficient."

Mark leaned in between the bucket seats and wiped a trickle of blood from the corner of his mouth. "You took your own sweet time getting there, Southern boy. They managed to get my gun and were going in for the kill. Cut it that close again and I'll kick your sorry butt all the way back to that alligator swamp you call home."

Nick stared at him in the rearview mirror. "No

spoon-fed Yankee momma's boy is going to kick anything of mine."

Heather glanced back and forth between them. They obviously knew each other, but she couldn't tell if they were teasing or about to slug each other. "Um, guys, are we okay here? What's going on?"

"What's going on," Nick said, shoving his car door open, "is that Rickloff's backup never showed. Which probably means there never *was* any backup."

Mark hopped over the side of the car and dusted off his shorts. "I hate to admit you were right, but you were. You saved our bacon back there."

Heather was still sitting in her seat, trying to follow their bizarre conversation, when Nick rounded the car to the passenger side, leaned over and scooped her up in his arms.

She was too surprised to do more than stare up at him as he carried her into the house.

Mark followed behind. He stopped just inside the kitchen, flipping on the lights, but Nick continued on into the living room with Heather.

"Um, Nick, I can walk. You can put me down."

He didn't bother answering and he didn't put her down. He used his shoulder to flip on the hall light and carried her all the way to the end into what must have been the master bedroom, based on the expansive size of the room. He kicked the door shut behind them and stopped beside the bed.

His brows were a dark, angry slash as he glared at her. The tightness around the corners of his eyes and the way he clenched his jaw told her she might be in as much trouble now as she had been back at the bar.

"Put me down." She tried to sound braver than she felt. The last time she'd seen him like this, he'd slapped her in handcuffs. She wasn't sure what to expect. She squirmed in his arms, anxious to get away from him.

He suddenly released her. She dropped to the bed and hadn't even stopped bouncing on the mattress before he came down on top of her.

The shock of his warm body pressed against hers had her mouth going dry. For a moment they just stared at each other. His body was rigid. His Adam's apple worked in his throat several times, as if he was struggling for words. Heat flooded through Heather, tightening her stomach. She was appalled that she was getting turned on, because it was quite obvious Nick wasn't suffering from the same affliction.

He looked as if he wanted to strangle her.

She didn't have to ask him why. She already knew. He was still furious that she'd jeopardized his career back at that nightclub in Saint Augustine and that she'd gotten him mixed up in this mess tonight. Although, really, it wasn't her fault. And he wasn't supposed to be here anyway. Was he? Actually, if she looked at it that way, he really didn't have a right to be angry at all. If anyone should be angry it was her, because he hadn't adequately warned her about the dangers. He should have tried harder to get her to *not* go along with Rickloff's plan. And just as soon as Nick quit glaring at her, she'd find the courage to tell him so.

"You could have been killed tonight." His voice shook.

Heather blinked in surprise. *That's* why he was upset? "You were *worried* about me?"

"Hell, yes, I was worried about you. You shouldn't have agreed to Rickloff's plan. I told you I didn't trust him, and you still insisted on plowing ahead. I'm on suspension. I'm supposed to be sitting at my house in my favorite recliner, which—I might add—is a hell of a lot more fun than being shot at. What do you think would have happened tonight if I hadn't disobeyed orders and come down here to keep an eye on you?"

She was pretty sure she wouldn't have survived the night without him, but she didn't think it was a good idea to say that out loud. He was already shaking, and from the tension in his body against hers, she guessed he was still fighting his own battle not to throttle her.

She swallowed hard. "I...ah...don't really know."

His mouth thinned and his eyes flashed. He shook his head and rolled off her to sit on the side of the bed, as if he couldn't stand to look at her anymore.

Heather scrambled up on her knees beside him, searching for the words that would ease his temper. She remembered he'd found humor in her thanking him repeatedly back in the car. She cleared her throat. "Thank you, again, Nick. Really. Thank you, a hundred times."

He closed his eyes briefly, still shaking his head.

She tried again. "I'm...ah...really grateful you

aren't sitting at home in your comfortable re-cliner."

He shot her an irritated look.

She sighed and straightened her legs, sitting on the edge of the mattress beside him. "Are you going to tell me how you ended up coming to our rescue? It sounded like you and Mark know each other, and that he was expecting you tonight."

He let out a long, deep breath. "When you refused my help, Rafe and I dug around and pulled some strings to get some information. When I found out that Mark was the agent you'd be working with down here, I contacted him. He and I used to work together out of the Fort Lauderdale office. He kept me posted on where you two were going to be. I rented this house because it was near enough to your motel and the bar to be useful, but far enough away and remote enough that it made a good hiding place if it came to that."

He twisted around to meet her gaze. "I borrowed a fast car in case I needed to make a quick getaway. Then I followed you two as closely as I could manage without being too obvious. I figured something was wrong when I never once ran into any other agents. If Rickloff was backing you up the way he was supposed to, someone should have challenged me earlier in the evening for keeping tabs on you two. No one ever did."

Heather scrambled off the bed and stood facing him. "I don't understand. Why wouldn't there be any backup? Rickloff's goal was to catch Gonzalez or some of his men when they swapped Lily for the cocaine."

He cocked a brow. "Rickloff's *goal* is to catch Gonzalez. Period. You're a pawn, and so is your sister. Don't forget that."

She wasn't sure she bought Nick's cynical version of what had happened. Surely a high-ranking DEA agent like Rickloff wouldn't be so cavalier with the safety of two civilians just so he could catch a drug dealer. There had to be another explanation for what had happened tonight.

"Why do you think Gonzalez didn't show?" she asked.

"Oh, I think he probably did. He just didn't let anyone see him. He would have come there to point you out to his men."

"What? Wait. What do you mean? We were there waiting to meet with him. We had the cocaine... Oh, my gosh. The cocaine! We lost it. If we don't have that cocaine we don't have anything to trade for Lily. What will we—"

He grabbed her arms. "Don't you get it yet? If Gonzalez was planning on a trade, he'd have shown himself. Tonight wasn't about a trade. Gonzalez set this meeting up for an entirely different reason."

"What reason is that?"

"He wanted you to come to Key West."

"But…I don't…" She twisted her fingers together in confusion. "Why would he want that?"

"For exactly the reason Rickloff said in the meeting yesterday. Gonzalez cares about Lily. He doesn't want to lose her. But he's a powerful man who maintains that power because people are afraid of him. If word gets around, and it will—it always does—that his mistress and her sister lost his drugs, or that either of them is helping the DEA, he'll lose face. He can't afford that. So he has to come up with an alternate plan. He wants to figure out how to save face in front of his men, but still keep Lily."

Heather nodded, trying to follow his reasoning. "Okay. And he cares about my sister, so hurting her is the last thing he'll do, right?"

"Based on the information I gathered last night and earlier today from my informants here in the Keys, yes. I think he really cares about her and he'll do whatever he can to protect her, as long as it doesn't mean giving up his reputation of power in front of his men."

Relief loosened the tightness in her chest. "Thank God. That means Lily is okay."

He stared at her for a long minute. "I don't think you've thought this through yet if you think things are going well here. Rickloff didn't back you up, even though he thought Gonzalez or his thugs would meet you at the bar. What does that tell you?"

She blinked in surprise as things started clicking together in her mind. "Rickloff is working for Gonzalez?"

He smiled, looking mildly amused at her conclusion. "No, I don't think so. From what Mark told me on the phone last night, Rickloff has an ego the size of the state of Florida. He's not the type to be at the beck and call of a drug dealer. He'd consider it beneath him. I believe he really does want to put Gonzalez in prison, partly to make the streets safer, but mainly because that would catapult his career to a higher level. At the least, he'd get a promotion. And if he has political aspirations, which Mark assures me Rickloff does, putting someone like Gonzalez away could be the perfect platform to put him in office."

"But Mark and I could have been killed."

He closed his eyes, his forehead wrinkling as if he were in pain. "Yes, you could have." When he looked at her again, there was tenderness in his eyes that reminded her of how he used to look at her. *Before.*

"We'll stay here tonight," he said. "I'll call the Key West DEA office and bring the special agent in charge, Dante Messina, up to speed on what's going on. He can run interference with the police about the shooting back in town, in case anyone called it in. Tomorrow morning, I'll take you to meet him and we'll get this all sorted out."

He gently pushed her hair out of her eyes. "Try

not to worry. Dante is far more reasonable than Rickloff. I've worked with him quite a bit this past year while on assignment down here. And I promise you I'll do everything I can to find your sister. Okay?"

She blew out a shaky breath. "Okay. I just hope she's—"

Red and blue lights suddenly lit up the room, flashing against the thin blinds covering the only window. Nick lifted Heather out of his way and ran to the window. She followed him, but he frowned at her and pushed her back as he lifted one of the slats to look out.

She caught a glimpse of a police car sitting in the driveway, pulled all the way up to the garage door. Both car doors opened and two policemen got out.

"I guess you were right," she said. "Someone in town must have reported the shooting and given a description of your car to the police."

Nick dropped the blinds back in place, shaking his head. "If they're the police, how did they find us?"

"Your car—"

"Is in the garage. They couldn't have seen it. And there aren't any other houses for miles around. That's why I chose this location. No one could have seen me pull the car into the garage."

Her fingernails bit into her palms. "So what are you saying?"

"What I'm saying is that I don't know what's going on. Maybe they're real cops, maybe they aren't. Maybe someone saw us when we made the turn down this road. They thought the cracked windshield looked suspicious so they called it in. Then again, maybe not."

He started to reach for the phone attached to his belt when a door slammed somewhere in the house.

His eyes widened. "Mark. No, damn it." He rushed around Heather and strode to the door.

"Stay here." He hurried into the hallway, firmly closing the door behind him.

Heather couldn't resist a quick peek through the blinds. The slamming door must have been Mark going out front, because he was now standing on the walkway talking to the two police officers. Heather clutched her hand to her throat, fervently hoping Nick's worries about the policemen were unfounded.

One of the policemen suddenly drew his gun and pointed it at Mark's chest. A gunshot rang out. Mark flipped backward onto the lawn.

Heather screamed. The policemen swiveled toward her, looking right at her.

She dropped the blind and flattened herself against the wall.

Oh, no, Mark. No, no, no.

Where was Nick? Was he already outside? Were they going to shoot him next?

Oh, no, please.

Muffled footsteps sounded through the house.

Heather clapped her hand over her mouth to keep from making any noise. Was that Nick? Or someone else?

Oh, God. Please let Nick be okay.

The footsteps pounded down the hallway, closer, closer. If that was Nick, wouldn't he have called out to warn her?

Heather whirled around. Nowhere to hide. She ran toward the door and lunged for the vase on the dresser as the door flew open. She swung the vase like a bat, aiming at her attacker's head.

The man's arm jerked up. The vase thunked against his forearm and fell to the floor, exploding into a dozen pieces.

Heather shoved at him and tried to escape through the doorway.

An iron grip clamped around her wrist and brought her up short.

"Heather, it's me," Nick's harsh whisper sounded near her ear. He flipped off the light switch, plunging the room into darkness.

She sagged against him, wrapping her arms around his waist, hugging him. "Nick, oh, my gosh. You're okay. They shot Mark. I thought you were outside, too, that they were going to shoot you."

"The men who shot Mark had disappeared by the time I made it to the front door." His voice was still a harsh whisper, as if he was afraid of making much noise. "They could be anywhere. We've got to get out of here."

He grabbed her wrist and pulled her down the hall toward the main room, forcing her to run to keep up with his long strides. He must have flipped the lights out when he ran to get her because the entire house was dark except for the moonlight filtering through the French doors off the back of the main room and through the skylights overhead.

"Can't we just grab Mark, get in the car and get out of here?" Heather whispered.

He peered out through the glass panes in one

of the back doors. "The police car is blocking the garage. I can't get the car out." He pulled out his cell phone. "Shade the screen to help conceal the light," he whispered.

She did as he said. "What are you doing?"

"Calling for backup." He pressed a button on the screen.

A soft "pfftt" sound echoed through the room. One of the glass panes in the French door next to them exploded.

Heather let out a startled yelp.

Nick pushed her down onto the floor. He aimed his gun toward the front of the house and fired off three quick shots. He shoved his phone in his pocket and threw open the door behind them.

"Come on." He grabbed Heather's wrist.

They took off running, with Nick pushing her ahead of him, using his body to block any attack from behind.

"What are we going to do?" Heather called back to him.

"Get to the woods," he said. "We'll use the trees for cover. I'll try to hold them off until we can get help."

They practically flew across the soft grass toward the woods behind the house.

Another shot rang out behind them.

Nick swore and pushed Heather harder. He fired a shot, then yanked Heather behind the first stand of oak trees.

HEATHER STARTED TO SLOW.

"Don't stop," Nick whispered harshly, urging her forward with his hand on her back. "Get to that next stand of trees. The bushes are thicker there, more cover." He had to get some distance between them and their pursuers.

When he thought they'd gone far enough, he pulled Heather to a stop. Her breathing was loud and choppy. He needed her to calm down, or anyone within ten yards of them would hear her breathing.

"Shouldn't you call for backup now?" she panted between breaths.

That last shot had shattered his phone holstered at his hip, but he wasn't about to tell her that. She was already so scared her face was ghost-white.

"In a minute," he said, trying to think of a lie that would make sense. "The screen is too bright. It will let our pursuers know right where we are."

She nodded, probably remembering the shot the last time he'd tried to use his phone. The person who'd shot the French door had a silencer, which told Nick far more about the men who were after them. They definitely weren't cops. And at least one of them was a highly paid assassin. The average drug dealer thug couldn't afford a silencer.

"Nick," Heather whispered, her breathing

slower and much more quiet now. "Mark is hurt. Shouldn't we try to go back and—"

He stared down at her. "I figured he was just playing dead for the gunmen, because he lost his gun back in town. He *was* wearing a Kevlar vest. And so are you. Right?" At her hesitation, his eyes narrowed. "Please tell me Rickloff didn't send you and Mark into that bar without bullet-resistant vests."

Heather blinked at him and swallowed hard. "I seem to remember him saying something about not being able to conceal a vest beneath T-shirts and shorts like tourists wear in the summer."

Nick swore viciously and shoved his gun back into his belt. He yanked his shirt over his head and threw it on the ground. He tugged at the Velcro straps of his vest, wincing when the ripping sound seemed to echo through the trees.

"What are you doing?" Heather shook her head when he lowered the vest over her head.

"Wait, you can't do this. You're the one who should be wearing this, not me."

Ignoring her pleas and her struggles, he tugged the straps, tightening them around her.

"No, stop it." She batted at his hands. "I am not going to be responsible for you getting hurt or killed. Stop it."

He grabbed her arms, holding her tight to stop her struggles. "Condition number two. Be quiet. And stop fighting me."

Heather instantly stilled but she continued to glare up at him. The woman was adorable when she was angry. Nick barely managed to squelch a threatening grin as he finished tightening the straps on the vest. He didn't want to give her the impression they were in the clear now and everything was okay.

Because they weren't, and everything was definitely *not* okay.

"Fine," she whispered. "I'll wear the vest, but

at least give me your backup gun. I'm an excellent shot. I can help."

He peered around the trees, watching for movement in the dark woods behind them. "What makes you think I have a backup gun?" he whispered.

"Because *you're* not the idiot who went into Satan's biker bar without a bulletproof vest. I'd bet my life, and I totally am, that you have a backup gun."

His mouth twitched and his gaze shot to hers.

The branch above them popped and cracked. Leaves and bark rained down on them. The assassin with the silencer must have spotted them and fired off a shot.

"No time," Nick whispered in a harsh voice. He grabbed Heather's right wrist with his left hand in an unbreakable viselike grip. "Come on. We're going to do the only thing we can do right now."

"What's that?"

"Run like hell."

Chapter Six

Nick pulled Heather behind a tree, holding her close as he scanned the woods around them. When he looked back down at her, the sick feeling in her stomach told her what he was about to say.

They were in serious trouble.

He held his finger to his lips in a shushing gesture. He held up one finger then pointed to their left. He held up two more fingers and pointed to their right.

Heather's heart stuttered in her chest as she realized what he was telling her. Two men on one side, one on the other. They were surrounded.

She nodded to let him know she understood. When they took off again, instead of pushing her in front of him, Nick held her glued to his side, guiding each of her steps, as if to ensure she didn't make any noise.

The sound of something snapping off to their right made Heather jump. She stumbled and stepped on a stick that snapped in two from her weight.

The large crack seemed to echo around them like a beacon. Nick tensed and froze, waiting, listening. A shout, something in Spanish, sounded off to their right. Nick took off, towing Heather with him, no longer trying to be quiet. They raced through the woods, hopping over fallen logs, dodging around trees as fast as they could go, trying to outrun their pursuers.

Heather cursed her short legs. She'd never cared before that she didn't have the long legs of a model. But right now she'd do anything for those longer strides so she wouldn't hold Nick back. If it weren't for her, he'd be perfectly safe. He wouldn't have given her his bulletproof vest and the men chasing them wouldn't be catching up.

Shouts sounded behind them. Footfalls pounded the ground.

Heather's breaths came in short pants. Nick was half dragging her along with him, forcing her to run faster than she'd even thought she could run. She knew she couldn't keep up this pace very long. The stitch in her side was already so painful she was clutching one hand against her ribs to try to keep going.

Ahead, moonlight glinted off the ocean, visible through breaks in the trees. In the daytime, Heather would have welcomed the sight. She longed to explore the thin, rocky, seashell-strewn strips of sand and clear blue-green water beyond. But seeing that water, inky-black in the night, get closer and closer, meant only one thing—they were trapped. With the ocean ahead and gunmen behind, there was nowhere else to go.

Nick shoved Heather behind a tree. He whirled around and squeezed off two shots into the woods behind them. A guttural scream of pain echoed through the woods.

"Vámonos, vámonos!" someone else, farther off, shouted in Spanish.

"Good grief, how many of them are there?" Heather whispered. She breathed in huge gulps of air, clutching her side.

Nick swiveled toward her. "Can you swim?" he asked, his voice low and urgent.

"I'm a Florida native. Of course I can—"

"Go." He waved toward the water visible through the trees. "Swim out about fifty feet. Then swim parallel to the shore, south, back toward town." He pointed toward his left.

She hesitated. "What about you? Aren't you coming with me?"

"I'll try to take out a few more of our pursuers

and lead them away from the water. I'll catch up with you. Just swim south." He gestured to the left again to make sure she knew the direction.

"Nick, I'm a good shot. Give me a gun."

He pressed his lips next to her ear. "I'm not willing to bet your life, or mine, on your marksmanship under pressure, not as long as there's a safer alternative. Now go."

A footstep sounded near them.

"Go," he mouthed, making a shooing gesture with his hand.

Heather fisted her hands in frustration. She whirled around and took off toward the ocean, stepping as quietly as she could, staying close to the trees for cover. Part of her was furious that Nick didn't trust her to help. But the other part was well aware of how even the most highly trained people—law enforcement officers, soldiers—were notoriously inaccurate with firearms when in a high-pressure situation. She had only ever fired at targets, and the shooting range certainly wasn't stressful in any way. Maybe Nick was right not to trust her ability to shoot in this type of situation. And if he was worrying about her, he couldn't adequately defend himself.

Crashing noises sounded in the woods, moving north and off to the east, away from her. Nick's plan was working.

Hating herself for leaving him, but knowing there wasn't much she could do without a gun, Heather lunged between the last two trees. She sprinted onto the narrow strip of sand. Her foot hit something hard and she went sprawling onto the ground. A conch shell. Heather shoved it away and climbed to her feet. She made her way more carefully to the water that was only a few feet away.

She didn't stop. She ran right into the warm water. When she was chest deep, she turned around to look back toward the beach. Thankfully, she didn't see anyone. Following Nick's orders, she swam farther out. Her waterlogged shoes kept trying to pull her down. She toed them off under the water and let them drop. She debated pulling off the vest, too, but she quickly discarded the idea. Nick had risked his life to give her the vest. She wasn't going to ignore his sacrifice by throwing the vest away.

The thought of him being shot sent a flash of panic straight through her. She stared back at the dark line of trees at the edge of the sand. What if he was hurt? What if he was lying in the bushes bleeding right now? Suddenly the fact that she'd been imprisoned in that filthy jail cell all weekend faded to insignificance. Nick had done what he'd done because it was his job. It wasn't fair for her to hate him for that, especially since his honor and protectiveness toward women were some of the very traits that had drawn her to him in the first place.

When they'd first met, it was on a beach very different from this one, back home. Nick had noticed a guy bothering her who didn't understand what "no" meant. He'd sent the other guy on his way. Then he'd grinned at her and called her darlin'. If any other guy had called her that she'd have thought he was being condescending. But there was nothing condescending about Nick. He was just pure Southern charm rolled up in a hot package, impossible to resist.

Every muscle inside her tightened at the thought of leaving him in those woods. She desperately wanted to go back and find him. But if she went back she could be a liability again, slowing him down, making him vulnerable.

No, she had to trust him and go along with his stupid conditions. He'd earned that trust a hundred times tonight, and she had to keep the faith that he knew what he was doing.

She drew a deep breath, then another, and submerged beneath the water, swimming farther out. When she thought she might be far enough from the shore, she rose, sticking her head out of the water just enough so she could breathe.

The tiny strip of sand that couldn't legitimately call itself a beach was still clear. No sign of her pursuers. But no sign of Nick, either.

Another shot rang out, startling her at how close it sounded. She drew a deep breath and submerged, swimming underwater again. She rose several more times for breaths and to make sure she was swimming in the right direction, parallel to shore. Each time she didn't see anyone. And each time she went right back under.

She hated condition number two, hated following Nick's orders unquestioningly. If they both survived this night, she was going to renegotiate his stupid conditions.

The next time she surfaced for air, she let out a small yelp before recognizing the figure swimming toward her. Nick. He quickly reached her with his powerful strokes. She would have thrown her arms around his neck with sheer joy that he was okay, but his grim expression held her back.

"Good job," he said. "You did great. You swam farther than I thought. We can cut back to shore now."

"What about the gunmen?"

"They're a good clip north of us, but the trail I laid won't fool them for long. They'll loop back to try to find us. We don't have much time. We need to get back to the house and take either the patrol car or my car, whatever works, and get out of here."

They struck out swimming side by side toward shore.

"How many were there? Were those cops after us, too?" Heather kicked her feet to try to keep up with him.

"I didn't see the supposed cops. But there were five men in the woods."

"Five?" Heather squeaked.

"Don't worry. I shot three of them. The odds are in our favor now."

"Oh, goodie," Heather grumbled.

Nick grinned. They were in the shallows now. He took her hand and pulled her with him back to shore and into the trees.

He stopped and squatted down by a twisted oak. He pulled his gun from under a pile of leaves where he must have put it before swimming out to get her. While he dusted off the dirt and grabbed whatever else he'd stored in the pile of leaves, Heather glanced anxiously around, keeping watch. Nick stood and grabbed her hand again, pulling her behind him through the woods. They rounded a clump of trees and suddenly they were on the front lawn of the house. Heather was surprised and relieved. She hadn't realized they were this close.

The police car was no longer parked out front. Had the fake cops left? Or had they just hidden their car to make Nick and Heather think they'd left?

Her breath caught in her throat as they ran past Mark's body, still lying on the grass. A reddish-brown stain darkened his shirt and spread down one side. She tugged her hand, trying to pull it out of Nick's grasp so she could stop and check on Mark.

Nick's fingers tightened around her wrist. He wouldn't let her stop. "Keep going."

The urgency in his voice had her pulse pounding in her ears. Had he seen something? Heard something? He pulled her at a dead run to the front door, then pressed her up against the side of the house, again using his body—his half-naked body, dressed only in jeans, *without* a bulletproof vest—to shield her. Heather wanted to scream at him and tell him how ridiculous and reckless he was being with his own safety, but she didn't want to distract him, so she stayed silent. For now.

He held up one finger to his lips again, then held his palm out telling her to wait. He crouched down with his pistol out and dove in through the open front door. An agonizing ten or fifteen seconds later, he pulled her inside. He shut and locked the front door, waved her to silence again and disappeared down the long hallway.

It was too dark to see many details, but Heather could see the back door was closed. They'd left it open when they ran out that same door earlier this evening. Or had they? Had Nick closed it just now, when he came inside, before he pulled her inside with him? Had he had enough time to do that?

Her throat tightened at the sound of running feet. Nick ran from the hallway into the living room. He ran past her in a whisper of sound, heading into the kitchen. A door creaked, footsteps sounded. Was that Nick? Or someone else making those sounds?

She inched her way back toward the front

door. Should she run for it? Go for help? Nick had said there weren't any other houses on this road. Where would she run? Back to the ocean?

She stopped. No, no, she couldn't run. She couldn't leave Nick, not again. If only she had a gun. She chewed her bottom lip. Nick didn't seem inclined to give her his backup gun. But did Mark have a backup gun? Had he mentioned that? She couldn't remember.

A noise sounded from the garage to her right. Her knees started to shake. She had to do something. She couldn't stand here waiting to be rescued, especially if Nick needed help. She squinted in the dim moonlight from the skylights. The end table by the couch had several statues on it. The dolphin statue looked heavy enough to crush a man's skull if she put all her weight behind it. The idea of actually hitting someone with it had her stomach churning, but if that's what it took to save Nick, she'd have to do it.

She pushed herself away from the wall and hurried to the statue before she lost her courage. Someone rushed into the room. Heather whirled around, lifting the statue before she recognized Nick's familiar silhouette.

He stopped in front of her, his white teeth flashing in the dark. "You can put the dolphin down," he teased. "The house is clear. I'm going to get Mark."

Heather clutched the heavy statue to her chest. It was the only weapon she had and she wasn't giving it up until Nick was safely back inside.

He opened the front door, holding his gun up at the ready. He leaned out before he ran outside, leaving the door cracked open behind him.

Heather rushed to the door and peered out. Nick was on the front lawn, crouching down next to Mark's body. He pressed his fingers against Mark's neck as if checking for a pulse. He hoisted him up on his shoulders and turned back toward the house. Thank goodness. Mark must still be alive or Nick wouldn't have risked his life to grab him.

Heather held the door open, closing and locking it after Nick came inside.

"I heard someone in the woods in the side yard," Nick whispered. "Get to the garage. Now. Go."

Her mouth went dry. She pitched the dolphin statue on the couch and led the way through the dark house, sorely wishing she could flip on a light. She held the door open to the garage so Nick could pass through with Mark.

"Is he going to be okay?" Heather asked.

"I don't know." His voice was tight, a harsh rasp full of pain and regret.

He rushed past her and heaved Mark over the side of the car into the backseat.

She ran to the passenger side of the car, stealing a quick look over the side at Mark. His chest rose and fell. He was still breathing, but just barely.

A muffled noise sounded from inside the house, followed by a dull thump.

Nick jerked his head toward the car, motioning for Heather to get in. He disappeared back into the house.

Heather bit the inside of her cheek to keep from calling out to him. What was he doing? She got into the car and turned in her seat, her gaze fastened on the dark maw of the open door that led into the kitchen.

Another thump sounded from inside the house, followed by a low moan.

Heather leaned over the side of the car, looking at the shelving for some kind of weapon. Why hadn't she kept the statue? She gasped when a dark shadow moved into the garage. Nick, again. The man was going to be the death of her the way he kept disappearing and re-appearing. She pressed her hand against her chest, her heart beating so fast she could hear it pulsing in her ears.

Nick gently eased the door to the house shut, dug his keys out of his pocket and ran to the car.

He jumped over the side and plopped down onto the driver's seat. "You said you wished you had a gun earlier. Just how good a shot are you?"

"I grew up on a farm. I've been shooting since I was ten. I guarantee I can outshoot you."

"Unfortunately, you just may have to prove that. The door to the house has hinges on the inside, meaning there's no way to brace it from out here." He laid his pistol in his lap and reached down, yanking up the leg of his jeans. A small holster was strapped to his calf. He pulled out a .38 snub-nose and handed it to her. "If anyone comes through that door, don't hesitate, shoot them."

She nodded, grateful to finally have a weapon, and turned around in her seat, aiming at the door that led back into the house.

The garage door squeaked as it began to rise. Heather swallowed hard. She felt so exposed knowing the door was opening behind her, but she kept her gun trained on the house door as Nick had told her to do.

The doorknob rattled. The door flew open. Heather didn't wait for someone to step out. She squeezed the trigger, aiming at the middle of the dark opening.

The shot was deafening in the confines of the garage. A man screamed and fell through the doorway onto the concrete floor behind the car.

"Hold on," Nick yelled.

Heather grabbed the back of her seat with her left hand as the car rocketed forward out of the garage. She kept her gun trained on the door to the house.

"Ah, hell. It's the freaking O.K. Corral around here. Get down," Nick yelled.

Heather dropped down into the seat.

Shots rang out behind them as the car flew down the driveway. Nick slid down in his seat, too, trying to take cover while steering the car.

The already cracked windshield shattered and sprayed bits of glass all over the inside of the car.

The car fishtailed into the road out front. Nick slid up higher in his seat and yanked the steering wheel hard left, then hard right. He punched the gas again.

Metal pinged as a bullet hit the back of the car. Nick gunned the car down the road. As soon as they rounded a curve, he sat straight up in his seat and wrestled the steering wheel to keep them from going into the ditch on the far side of the road. The car straightened out and practically flew down the narrow two-lane road back toward town.

When the car quit swerving, Heather stowed her gun in the console and climbed into the backseat.

"What are you doing?" Nick demanded.

"Checking on Mark."

"Hang on, I'm turning."

She held on to the back of the seat in front of her as Nick swerved onto a side road, tires screeching. He continued his mad dash, flying down street after street, passing more and more houses as they got closer to town.

"How's he doing?" Nick asked, turning onto another road, but at a less-frantic speed than before.

Heather pulled Mark's shirt open and found the entry hole in his chest, about halfway down his rib cage on the right side. She pressed her hands against his injury, applying pressure. "The bleeding isn't that bad now, but he's still unconscious. We have to get him to a doctor."

"Check his pockets for his phone. Mine is… waterlogged."

Heather wondered why he hadn't hidden his phone, just like he'd hidden his gun, to keep it dry when he swam out after her. He must have forgotten. She kept one palm pressed against Mark's wound while she fished into his pockets. When she found his cell phone, she pressed a button and was relieved that the light came on and five bars showed they had service. "You want me to call 911?"

"No. Call this number instead." He rattled off a phone number and Heather punched it in.

She handed him the phone, then pressed both palms against Mark, trying to stop the bleeding.

Nick spoke in some kind of DEA combination of code words that made no sense to her. When he hung up, he set the phone in the console next to his gun.

"We're ten minutes from the hospital. Backup's on the way."

"You sure about that?" she asked. "I don't remember backup working out so well the last time."

She saw his quick grin in the rearview mirror. She didn't think she'd ever met someone before who could smile or laugh so much when people were trying to kill him. She had a feeling he might have actually enjoyed tonight if she hadn't been there to slow him down or force him to have to protect her instead of going after the bad guys.

Some of the tension drained out of her shoulders. Maybe the worst was over now. Maybe they really would make it out of this mess alive.

"You were right," she called out over the sound of the wind rushing by. "About everything. I should have trusted you back in Saint Augustine when you warned me about Rickloff's plan."

His grin faded and his jaw tightened. "You've got nothing to apologize for. You were put in an impossible situation. You're a civilian. You never should have been given the choices Waverly and Rickloff gave you."

"I realize that now." She shoved her wet hair out of her face. "But there's still the question of what to do about my sister. I don't even know if she's alive."

"We'll figure something out. Trust me."

"I do."

He gave her a sharp look in the mirror before looking back at the road.

Heather wasn't sure what that look meant, but she was willing to bet it had something to do with *him* not trusting *her.* Since her arrest at the nightclub, she and Nick had never sat and discussed what had happened. Would it make a difference in his feelings toward her if they sat down and talked? Or would he even give her a chance to explain her side?

A few minutes later, the squeal of tires sounded behind them. Nick checked the mirrors. Heather jerked around in her seat. A car had just swerved from a side road and was rapidly gaining on them. The headlights blinked three times.

Heather half stood, holding on to the back of Nick's seat for balance. She reached for the snub-nose she'd left in the console.

Nick grabbed her hand before she could get

the gun. "Hold on, Annie Oakley. Those aren't the bad guys. That's our backup."

She plopped back down, grinning over his Annie Oakley comment. Either she was too exhausted and relieved that backup had arrived to think clearly anymore, or his warped sense of humor was contagious.

Minutes later, as promised, they were at the hospital. Nick pulled up to the emergency room entrance. The backup car pulled right up behind them and two men jumped out. They both wore wrinkled shirts and jeans, as if they'd pulled on whatever clothes they could find when Nick's call came in. They immediately flanked Heather.

Nick scooped Mark up out of the backseat and preceded them in through the emergency room doors. A nurse saw them and her eyes widened with alarm. She ran around her desk and grabbed a wheelchair. Nick set Mark in the chair and braced him so he wouldn't fall out.

One of the agents put his hand on Mark's shoulder, anchoring him to the chair. "I've got this."

Nick nodded his thanks, and the agent rushed off with the nurse and Mark through the swinging doors into the heart of the emergency room.

Nick introduced himself and Heather to the remaining agent, who said his name was Tanner, and that the other agent who'd gone with Mark was named Chuck.

Another nurse stopped next to them and handed Nick a hospital gown to replace the shirt he'd left in the woods when he'd given Heather his vest. He murmured a thank-you and shrugged the gown on as he spoke to Tanner.

Heather was surprised at how much blood was smeared on Nick's abdomen. Mark must have bled all over him when Nick picked him up out of the backseat. She quietly offered up a quick prayer for Mark's safety and tuned back in to what Nick and Tanner were saying.

It soon became clear they had never met each other before.

"Wait. Nick, you don't know this man but you called him for backup?" she asked.

"I called the satellite office here in Key West and asked for help. Tanner and Chuck were bar-hopping nearby so they answered the call."

Tanner rolled his eyes. "We were working, not barhopping." He waved his hand at his clothes. "It may not look that way, but half my job involves dressing down to blend in."

Heather smiled at him. "I understand. I do that a lot, too."

"You're DEA?"

"Oh, no. I'm a private investigator. But half the time I either meet prospective clients in bars or end up meeting informants in bars. It's an unfortunate downside to my job."

"Ah." He didn't look impressed, and Heather felt her face grow warm with embarrassment.

She probably seemed like a bumbling amateur to an experienced DEA agent.

"Don't worry, ma'am," Tanner said. "We'll take good care of both of you. Let's go find somewhere a bit less out in the open and figure out what's going on."

"Go ahead. I'll catch up," Nick said. "I'm going to check on Mark." He hung back while Tanner led Heather down the hall.

"Wait a minute." Heather stopped and turned around. Nick was going to let her out of his sight, with an agent he'd only just met? Knowing how protective he was, that didn't sit right with her. She stared at him suspiciously.

He raised a brow in question and crossed his arms over his chest. That action made the hospital gown mold to his body. Heather's eyes widened and she gasped in shock.

A growing red stain saturated the part of

the gown covering Nick's lower left side. That wasn't Mark's blood.

It was Nick's.

Chapter Seven

Nick plucked at the fresh hospital gown, hating the necessity of wearing the darn thing. His jeans, lying on the emergency room countertop beside the bed he was sitting on, were bloody where the bullet had scraped across his hip. He didn't relish the idea of putting the jeans back on, but he couldn't exactly walk out in the flimsy gown he'd worn while the doctor had sewn him up.

A knock sounded on the door. Before he could say anything, the door flew open. Heather stood there, her two DEA agent shadows standing behind her. Two more agents had arrived a few minutes ago and were guarding Mark, just in case someone came in the hospital to seek him out and finish what they'd started.

"Give us a minute, okay, guys?" Heather called over her shoulder. She didn't wait for an answer. She shoved the door shut, tossed a small bag onto the countertop and put her hands on her hips. Her deep blue eyes were practically shooting sparks as she glared at him.

Nick's curiosity about what was in the bag was no competition for the vision standing in front of him. He couldn't have moved to pick up that bag if he'd wanted to. He was too busy just trying to draw a normal breath.

He crossed his arms and tried to appear unaffected, but boy did she look good. Someone had given her a fresh white T-shirt and jeans, both a size too small by some standards but pretty near perfect by his. Every curve was outlined for his hungry gaze. He swallowed, hard, and reluctantly dragged his gaze up from her generous breasts.

"Is there a problem?" he asked, barely able to get the words out past his tight throat. He swallowed again and reminded himself she was off-limits. She wasn't his girlfriend, not anymore, not if he wanted to keep his job. He'd have a hard enough time as it was explaining to Waverly how he'd ended up in Key West in a firefight when he was suspended and was supposed to be in Saint Augustine.

"You got shot," Heather accused.

"Uh, yeah. A little bit."

"A little bit?" she choked out. "Why didn't you tell me you were hurt?"

"We were busy trying to escape without getting killed."

She shook her head and fisted her hands at her sides. Her gaze went to the items sitting in the tray next to his bed. Her eyes widened and her mouth fell open.

He probably should have hidden his phone.

She strode toward him and grabbed his ruined phone from the tray. When she held the twisted piece of metal up, the bullet hole was clearly visible. Her eyes flashed daggers at him as she tossed the phone back onto the tray. "Water-logged, Nick? You said your phone was water-logged."

"I'm pretty sure I said it was broken." She sure looked good when she was angry. Her skin was flushed a delicate pink. Her long hair flew out around her and her breasts pushed against her too-tight shirt as she put her hands on her hips.

Nick clutched the edge of the bed to keep from reaching for her.

She narrowed her eyes. "No, you said the phone was waterlogged. You *implied* you forgot to leave your phone on the beach with your gun when you went into the ocean. I thought that was odd for you to forget something like that. Now I know you didn't. You lied to me."

He shrugged, unimpressed by that accusation. He lied all the time. It was his job. If lying meant keeping her from worrying and keeping her safe, that's what he would do. "I didn't want you to worry about an insignificant injury."

"Insignificant? You call a gunshot insignificant?"

"Through and through. A handful of stitches." He gave her his best frown when what he really wanted to do was pull her against him and remind himself how well her curves fit against his hard planes. There was only one reason he could think of for her to be this upset. She still cared about him. After the way he'd treated her, that surprised him. And pleased him. Blood started pumping to a part of his body that left his brain slightly dazed from lack of oxygen.

"I could have helped you," she insisted. "When did you get shot?" She reached past him, tore the plastic bag open that she'd carried in and dumped out a pair of jeans, a shirt, and miraculously, a pair of tennis shoes that looked like they just might fit.

She grabbed the blanket from the foot of the bed and tossed it over his lap. Then she began tugging at the fastenings on his hospital gown, apparently intent on helping him change clothes. He wondered just how far she'd go with that, and he couldn't seem to dredge up any desire to refuse her help.

She pulled the gown off and pitched it on the countertop. "Well? When did you get shot?"

He had a feeling if he told her he'd gotten shot just as they'd reached the woods after running from the house, that she'd never let him hear the end of it. He decided a vague reply was the safer route. "I'm not really sure. It didn't even hurt."

Actually, it had hurt like hell, but he wasn't going to admit it.

She rolled her eyes and helped him slide his arms into the clean shirt. "*I'm* sure that it did. I don't buy for one second that you don't know when you were hit." She stepped back, apparently deciding he could button his own shirt, and raked her hands through her hair.

"I'm tougher than I look," she said. "I don't want you giving up your Kevlar vest for me and running into a firefight. And if I'd known you were injured, I could have helped, somehow. I could have dressed the wound to make sure you didn't lose too much blood, for one thing. I have enough on my conscience without adding you to the list."

"Like what?" He didn't bother with the top two buttons on his shirt. He grabbed the fresh jeans and lifted a leg to put them on.

Heather's eyes widened and she whirled around. "What do you mean, like what?" she asked.

Nick smiled at her sudden nervousness and tossed the blanket back on the bed to make it easier to pull on his pants. "You said you had enough on your conscience. Like what, for instance?"

He pulled the clean jeans on, wincing when they tugged on his stitches. The fact that he was partly turned on from ogling Heather's breasts and staring at her curvy backside didn't help with the snug fit. He was extra slow and careful with the zipper, since he was forced to go commando.

She threw her hands in the air. "What do I have on my conscience? Really? Everything! Mark being hurt. You being hurt. And Lily, God knows it's my fault she's in this mess."

Nick stilled. "What do you mean it's your fault?"

She peeked over her shoulder, as if to make sure nothing was exposed that shouldn't be before turning around to face him.

Good grief, the woman was adorable. She acted as if she'd never seen him naked before. Then again, they'd only slept together once, the night before the raid on the club. And speaking for himself, one time with the little firecracker wasn't enough, not even close. It would have to be, of course, which meant he'd probably spend the rest of his life wanting her and wondering what could have been.

That thought had his mood taking a dive south.

He grabbed his wallet from the tray and shoved it into his pants pocket. "How is it your fault that Lily's in this mess?" he repeated.

A knock sounded on the door.

"Come in," Nick called out. He didn't miss the look of relief that crossed Heather's face. He made a mental note to ask her that question again later, when they were alone.

Chuck and Tanner stepped inside.

"About ready?" Tanner asked.

"Just about." Nick sat back on the bed and grabbed the pair of shoes. "How's Mark doing?"

"He's still in surgery," Chuck said. "But the doctor said his prognosis is good. We'll keep agents guarding his room until he's stable enough to be transferred to a Miami hospital."

Heather stepped forward and pushed Nick's hands away. She grabbed one of his shoes and gently slid it onto his foot. He stared at her in surprise. It had been hurting like crazy trying to bend down to put his shoes on, so he appreciated her help. But he couldn't fathom why she was being so nice and concerned after he'd left her in jail all weekend. He owed her an apology, at the least, and here she was trying to take care of him.

He thanked her and forced his attention back to Tanner. "Did you find the men who were after us?"

"Not yet, but we did find the police car. It was stolen right out of a parking lot earlier tonight. Pretty bold. And it proves this whole thing was planned. Nothing spur-of-the-moment about it, that's for sure."

Heather finished tying Nick's shoes and

stepped back. "How will I know the real cops from the fake cops when I go back to my motel?"

"You're not going back to that motel," Nick said. "Gonzalez's men will be watching, hoping you'll return."

"But my suitcase, my clothes—"

"We've got that covered, ma'am," Tanner spoke up. "We've already had someone pick up your things. And as soon as the police release the crime scene at the house you rented," he said, addressing Nick, "we'll get your stuff from the house. But that might be a while. In the meantime, give me a list of what you'll need and I'll send someone to a store to get it."

"Thanks. I appreciate that. I assume you'll put Heather and me up at a hotel in town tonight?"

At Chuck's nod, he continued. "You said the police are processing the scene. Were they able to identify the men I shot in the woods behind the house? And the one Heather shot in the garage?"

Heather shivered and wrapped her arms around her waist. She might think she was tough, and maybe she was, but obviously the idea of shooting someone—no matter how much they deserved it—didn't sit right with her. Nick hated that she'd had to experience that. No matter how many times he was forced into that kind of situation, it still ate at him every time he had to hurt someone or take a life. Heather wasn't in law enforcement. She hadn't signed up for that kind of burden. Waverly and Rickloff deserved a special place in hell for using her and abandoning her when she needed their protection.

Tanner and Chuck stared at him in surprise. "Are you saying you shot someone? Both of you?"

"Yes," Nick answered slowly, studying them both. "I shot two men back in town who were trying to kill Mark. I shot three more in the woods and Heather shot one in the garage. It's possible they weren't all killed and some of them got away before the police got there." He glanced back and forth between them. "Are you telling me no one found *any* bodies?"

Tanner shook his head. "Not a one. They did find blood in the garage, but they figured it was Mark's. How certain are you that you actually hit anyone?"

Nick crossed his arms, insulted they'd even asked. "I never miss."

"Neither do I," Heather said, crossing her arms as well and looking just as insulted as Nick felt.

Tanner motioned to Chuck, who nodded and pulled his phone out of his pocket as he stepped out of the room.

"We'll notify the police to make another sweep, see if they can find a blood trail in the woods. But that may not be possible until daylight."

"Put the hospital on alert for gunshot victims and make sure they notify the DEA if anyone comes in for treatment," Nick said.

Tanner nodded. "Will do. We've already set up hotel rooms for the night under some aliases. You two will be in a two-bedroom suite. Chuck and I will be in the room next door, just a phone call away or a knock on the wall if you need us. Tomorrow morning we'll take you to our office. Our boss wants to debrief you on everything that happened."

"Have you spoken to Waverly or Rickloff?" Nick asked.

"We spoke to Rickloff. He claims there was a miscommunication, a mix-up about the name of the bar. He claims his men wanted to provide backup but didn't know where to go."

"A miscommunication?" Nick said. "That's what they call it these days?"

"Call what?" Heather asked.

Incompetence. Actually, he was beginning to wonder if Heather's original suspicions about Rickloff were right, that he might be working for Gonzalez. But he wasn't going to air that thought in front of fellow agents without facts to back it up.

"Never mind," he said, in response to Heather's question. He eyed Tanner. "Since this is the only hospital in Key West and the men who tried to kill us know we grabbed Mark, it's a pretty safe bet they'll assume we're here, too. I bet they've already got someone watching this place. We can't just walk out the front doors."

"We can take you through the ambulance bay."

Nick shook his head. "Not good enough. This was a well-planned attack with plenty of manpower and a cleanup crew, or else you'd have found the bodies." He slid a glance at Heather. "They didn't get what they came for. *You.* So I'm betting they're not going to just say forget it. They'll be worried we'll go into hiding, so they won't want to miss us leaving the hospital. They'll watch everyone who comes in or out."

"Then what are we supposed to do?" Heather glanced worriedly back and forth.

"Does this hospital have a medevac helicopter?" Nick asked.

Tanner shook his head. "No. When we have trauma cases, Ryder Trauma Center in Miami sends their chopper to airlift the victims. That's an hour out, and they won't send the medevac for something like this." He grinned and pulled his phone out. "But I do know where we can get a chopper."

HEATHER TUCKED THE last of her hair up underneath the ball cap and critically inspected her reflection in the hospital bathroom mirror. The T-shirt hugged her chest almost indecently. And the jeans were snug, too. The nurse who gave Heather her clothes had been just a little smaller than Heather. The sneakers were tight, too, but at least she wouldn't trip over her own feet when she ran outside. Would Gonzalez's men recognize her in this outfit? It certainly didn't conceal much, other than her hair.

"Heather," Nick's deep voice called through the door. "The chopper's a minute out. We need to hurry."

She tugged at her T-shirt, trying to stretch it out some more, but gave up. She sighed and opened the bathroom door.

Nick stood in the opening. He swallowed, his Adam's apple bobbing in his throat. "You're not going to fool anyone in that outfit, even with the ball cap," he said, his voice oddly tight.

"What choice do I have?"

"I'll grab you a lab coat on the way out."

He'd been luckier than her at getting clothes that fit. He'd rolled the sleeves of the dress shirt up to his elbows, giving him a rakish, sexy appeal that had Heather clutching her hands into fists to keep from reaching for him. No one should look that good after the horrible night they'd just experienced.

Thinking about the men possibly watching

the hospital, she shivered. The night and all its dangers were far from over.

Whump. Whump. Whump. The sound of the helicopter's blades sounded overhead.

Nick automatically glanced up, as if he could see the helicopter through the ceiling. "Chopper's here. Let's go."

Heather stepped out of the bathroom, her borrowed sneakers painfully squeezing her feet.

"This way." Nick led her out the door and down the hall to their left.

They could hear the sound of excited voices coming from the front of the hospital. Having a helicopter touch down in the parking lot was definitely not the norm. The DEA agents had cleared the lot right in front of the emergency room doors to make space for the chopper.

"Come on," Nick urged, pulling Heather with him to the exit. "We have to time this just right." He held the door open, and Heather ran with him outside, to the parking lot out back.

Less than a minute later, Nick drove their borrowed car down the side road next to the hospital. Heather leaned over in the passenger seat to look out Nick's window. "Fake Nick" and "fake Heather," both DEA agents from the Key West office, wearing exactly what Nick and Heather had been wearing when they got to the hospital, ran out of the emergency room doors and into the waiting chopper—a chopper that had *Bubba's Seafood* written on the side.

That explained Tanner's grin when he said he could get a helicopter.

Heather wouldn't have believed for one second that the shirtless man pretending to be Nick was really Nick. Nick's abs were much more defined and his biceps were twice as big.

"Do you think we fooled Gonzalez's men?" she asked.

"I sure as hell hope so." Nick punched the accelerator and the car leaped forward.

Chapter Eight

A knock on the hotel room door had Nick waving Heather into the first bedroom. He drew his gun and leaned back against the wall.

"Who is it?" he called out.

"Tanner."

Nick leaned over and looked through the peephole before unlocking the door. Tanner hurried inside and Nick locked the door behind him.

Heather stepped out from the bedroom without waiting for Nick to give the all clear. He barely resisted the urge to remind her of condition number two as he holstered his gun. The only reason he didn't was because he didn't want to embarrass her in front of the other agent. But she was going to have to learn to be more careful. What would she have done if it hadn't been Tanner at the door?

He shook his head and waved Tanner over to the couch.

"How did it go?" Nick asked.

"Hard to say. We didn't notice any vehicle activity on the ground when the chopper took off, other than your car leaving the hospital. The agents tailing you didn't see anyone else following. I'm not sure what to think. Either Gonzalez didn't have anyone watching and we went totally overboard getting that chopper—which, I might add, is going to be fun to explain on my next expense report—or he's a lot smarter than I thought."

"I've never met the man in person, but I've met plenty who have while I was building my undercover identity this past year," Nick said. "He's got a reputation for being on top of things and isolating himself behind layers of front men. If his thugs were the ones after Heather and me, I guarantee they were watching the hospital."

Heather plopped down on the opposite couch. "If? What are you saying? That Gonzalez might not have been the one who went after us?"

"I'm just open to all possibilities until proven otherwise," Nick said. "Tanner, have your men interviewed any witnesses who saw the shoot-out near the bar?"

"We're still canvassing that area. No witnesses yet, but that's no surprise in that part of town. The drug trade has a wrap on that area."

"What about my sister?" Heather asked. "Has there been any word about her? Other than the note from the men who abducted her, I haven't heard anything. I don't even know if…if she's alive."

"I'm new to this case," Tanner said. "Can't say that I really have much background, other than what Nick gave me in the hospital. But I *can* tell you that your sister and Gonzalez have been an item for quite some time. If it makes you feel better, I seriously doubt he'll hurt her if he can avoid it. That's not what he wants at all. The fact that he went after you with so much man-power, and that he didn't even seem interested in the duffel bag of drugs, tells me he's trying to make a public statement. And stealing a po-lice car on top of everything else, well, that's definitely out of character for him. He doesn't normally tangle directly with law enforcement. He's got too much to lose."

"I'm not sure I understand," she said.

Nick scooted forward on the couch opposite from her and rested his forearms on his knees. "What Tanner is saying is that if Lily were dead, Gonzalez would have no reason to go after you. The fact that he did go after you is a good indi-cation that he's still trying to figure out a way to save face and prove that he's still in control of his empire. Plus, if he killed Lily, he'd dump her body…"

He cursed his poor choice of words when Heather blanched and wrapped her arms around her waist.

"I'm sorry," he said. "I was just trying to say that if your sister was dead, we'd know about it. Gonzalez wouldn't try to hide what he'd done. Just the opposite. He'd want everyone to know that the woman who'd stolen from him had paid the ultimate price, as a warning to others."

She nodded, some of the color returning to her face. "I hope you're right, that she's unharmed."

Nick exchanged a glance with Tanner. The worried expression on Tanner's face told Nick they were both thinking the same thing.

Lily might not be dead, but "unharmed" was a stretch.

Even if Gonzalez eventually let Lily go, a man like him wasn't going to ignore the fact that his mistress had stolen from him, which was exactly what Nick's informants had basically confirmed when he'd arrived this morning. The rumor was that Lily had gotten into a fight with Gonzalez and took off with the kilos.

Nick figured the odds were about seventy-thirty that Lily had already experienced Gonzalez's wrath, and that her suffering wasn't going to end until—if—she was rescued.

HEATHER WAS STILL exhausted the next morning when Nick dragged her out of bed at the unholy hour of seven o'clock. But fear for her sister had her quickly showering and getting dressed without complaint. They'd rushed over to the Key West DEA office, and now she was sitting in the lobby, doing nothing but watching the seconds on the clock tick by while Nick met with Dante Messina, the special agent in charge.

Why she wasn't being included in that meeting made no sense to her. Lily was her sister, after all, and both of their futures were on the line. Those two facts should have ensured that she was allowed inside the DEA "hallowed offices" instead of relegated to the lobby with Tanner and Chuck babysitting her. She wasn't sure if they were really worried about her safety or whether their job was to make sure she didn't run away. She didn't get the feeling these DEA agents trusted her any more than Nick did.

The clock on the wall showed that Nick had been gone for over half an hour. Heather let out a deep sigh.

Chuck looked up from the newspaper he was reading in the chair across from her. "Are you sure you don't want anything, Miss Bannon? I can send Tanner out for Starbucks or Mickey D's."

Tanner, sitting next to Chuck, cocked a brow. "Or I can send Chuck out to get whatever you need."

His quick glance at the door to the other room told Heather he was just as anxious as she was to find out what was going on. Heather vaguely wondered what Chuck and Tanner had done to draw the short straw and be stuck in the lobby with her.

Before she could tell them she didn't want anything, the door opened.

Heather jumped to her feet, expecting to see Nick. Instead, Dante Messina—whom she'd met briefly when they first arrived—strode out of the room and stopped in front of her.

"Miss Bannon," he said. "Thank you for waiting. We're ready for you now." He held his hand out toward the open doorway.

"Thank you." Heather preceded him into the room and Dante followed behind.

As soon as she stepped inside, she stopped and stared in amazement.

Dante moved past her and spoke in low tones to three men standing beside one of the computer monitors on the left side of the room.

"Impressive, isn't it?"

Heather jerked around at the sound of Nick's voice. He was standing beside her, grinning as if everything were perfectly fine. As if none of the horrible events yesterday had ever happened. Then she noticed the tiny lines around his eyes, the tension in his stance. Nick wasn't fine at all. He looked…worried.

"It *is* impressive," she answered. "I've never seen anything like it."

"Neither have I. And I've been in a lot of DEA offices around the country. I have to admit I've got a bad case of technology envy right now."

Heather could understand why. This office was unlike anything she'd ever seen, except maybe in a movie. There were no cubicle walls. The entire room was open, with three enormous semicircular tables that stretched from one side to the other, in tiers, all facing the front like stadium seating in a theater, or maybe a NASA control room. Agents sat at the various workstations, talking into headsets or typing at their state-of-the-art computers. An electronic map of the Florida Keys was currently displayed on the screen at the end of the room, with live pictures of different parts of the Keys being flashed down the left side.

Dante finished his conversation with the three men he was with and waved at Nick and Heather to join them.

"Come on," Nick said, resting his hand on the small of Heather's back. "That's our cue."

They headed down the stairs and went through a side door with Dante and the three other agents. Though smaller than the room they'd just come from, this office had the same theater-style screen on the far wall, showing the same live shots.

Dante didn't sit behind the desk that dominated one side of the room. Instead, he and his agents sat in the well-worn group of chairs arranged in a circle in front of the desk. Heather couldn't imagine Nick's boss giving up his position of power by sitting with his agents like Dante. Nick led Heather to one of the chairs and sat beside her. He squeezed her hand as if to reassure her, then let go.

"These men are my section leaders," Dante said, directing his comments to Heather.

He introduced each man and Heather shook their hands.

"I'm sorry I left you waiting so long," Dante apologized. "But I had to gather some facts together and hear Nick's side of what happened before I spoke to you."

"No problem." She glanced worriedly at Nick. He gave her a reassuring nod.

Dante rested his forearms on his knees. "I understand you and your sister were arrested for possession of cocaine, with intent to sell."

Heather jerked back in her chair as if she'd been slapped.

"I'm not judging you," Dante assured her. "I'm fact-finding so I can make some decisions."

"Fine. The *facts* are that my sister had cocaine in her possession because she's mixed up with a drug-dealing boyfriend who took advantage of her vulnerability. I tried to destroy the drugs to keep her from using them or from doing something worse, as you said, like selling them." She directed her next statement to Nick. "I'm not a drug dealer."

Nick's eyes widened. His reaction told Heather he'd never considered that she was. Well, it would have been nice if he'd bothered to tell her that. She crossed her arms and faced Dante.

"The boyfriend you're referring to is, of course, Jose Gonzalez," Dante continued. "He's a major trafficker of cocaine through the Keys to Miami, and on to other cities like Saint Augustine. Nick tells me that Waverly offered you a deal, that if you helped him get Gonzalez he'd drop all charges against you and your sister. I have a problem with that, because Gonzalez is on my turf. Rickloff is out of the Miami office and never consulted me. If he had, I wouldn't have offered you a deal."

Heather shot a desperate look at Nick, but she couldn't read the hard expression on his face. What was going on?

"I don't understand. I signed an agreement. I was sent here with Agent Watkins…" She swallowed hard against the tightening in her throat and flushed with guilt because Watkins had been injured, but she plowed ahead. "I did exactly what I was told. I'm cooperating in every way that I can."

He held up his hand to stop her. "I'm not nullifying your deal. I can't. It's legal and binding. I'm just saying that I agree with Nick. It was a bad deal, a lousy idea, and if anyone had consulted me—which they didn't—I would have explained to them how stupid it was."

"I don't understand," Heather said.

"As far as I'm concerned, Waverly is responsible for Watkins being hurt and for you and

Nick almost being killed. Not to mention, he didn't provide backup. Rickloff isn't an idiot. He knew what would happen. I can only conclude one thing. He wanted Gonzalez to abduct you."

Heather's hand flew to her throat. "That's insane."

"No, that's desperation. Rickloff has been after Gonzalez for a long time, with no more success than I've had. He wants to get him, badly, so that blinded him to the dangers. I can't imagine he wanted you hurt. There's nothing to gain by that. But it's logical to assume if Gonzalez's men grabbed you they'd have taken you back to one of his private compounds. Rickloff wanted to follow you to that compound to capture Gonzalez."

He stood, picked something up off his desk that appeared to be a remote control and crossed to the screen on the far wall. The pictures changed, revealing a more detailed map of the Keys, with several red Xs on it. He waved his hand to encompass the entire screen. "Gonzalez has dozens of homes throughout the Keys and south Florida. Most are protected like military compounds, with the latest security gadgets and a full staff of security guards. There are some remote houses, too, on smaller islands, basically little blips of land just a mile or so across that you won't see on most maps. Gonzalez likes to go from compound to compound like a game of musical chairs, because he knows we're watching. The problem is, he has several look-alikes, much like Saddam Hussein had in Iraq. We're never quite sure where the real Jose Gonzalez is at any particular time. It's an old-school trick, but effective."

He tossed the remote back on his desk and sat down again. "We really don't know which house Gonzalez thinks of as his real home, which brings me to my point. We have no way of figuring out where your sister is without searching every compound, every little island he owns. No judge is going to give us a warrant to do that, and Rickloff knows that. I believe he was hoping to get Gonzalez to kidnap you so he could follow you to where Lily was being held. Armed with that information, he could get a search warrant. I'm sure he thought it would be a simple in-and-out procedure, no one gets hurt. But, as usual, he underestimated Gonzalez."

Heather stared at the map. All those Xs made her slightly nauseous. Finding Lily was starting to look like an impossible task. "But if what you're saying is true, about all those compounds, how would Rickloff have known where to go if Gonzalez kidnapped me?"

Dante twisted sideways in his chair to pick up something from his desk. He held it out in his palm—the parrot transmitter Mark was wearing on his shirt in the bar.

"This isn't just a microphone," Dante said. "It's also a homing beacon. I believe Rickloff planned to use that to find you after you were taken. Since Mark was still wearing the pin when he was taken into the E.R., the nurse who cut off his clothes put this in the bag that contained his belongings. That bag was put in his room. None of my agents noticed the pin or realized what it was until there was an attempt on Mark's life this morning at the hospital. Even though we had him sequestered in a remote room under a fake name, one of Gonzalez's men found him and tried to kill him."

"Oh, no. Is he…okay?" Heather asked, her nails biting into her palms.

"Yes. Fortunately we had him well guarded, but the man who tried to kill him was killed in the scuffle, so we couldn't get any additional information out of him. Regardless, my point is that Rickloff made some terrible mistakes. I could have told him what outcome to expect if he paraded you in public for Gonzalez's men to see. Rickloff and Waverly may make deals, but Gonzalez doesn't. Your sister—"

"Lily."

He nodded. "Lily. She's been living with Gonzalez for a while. She—"

"Wait, wait," Heather said. "Everyone keeps saying my sister was Gonzalez's girlfriend. Now you're saying they were living together. You just showed me that he owns entire islands. That means he's wealthy, right?"

Dante frowned, not looking pleased at her interruption. "Yes. He's quite wealthy actually. He owns many legitimate businesses that we believe he uses to launder his drug money. But yes, he's rich."

"Does he normally spend money on the women he associates with? Does he buy them cars, clothes, things like that?"

"Of course."

"Then why did my sister show up in Saint Augustine a couple of weeks ago flat broke, driving a car that wouldn't even start the night we were arrested?"

The room went silent. Heather looked at each man, including Nick, waiting for someone to answer her, but no one did. "None of you have thought about that?"

"It's a valid question," Nick finally said. "One wouldn't expect that Gonzalez's mistress would have a rattletrap car and no spending money. I have no idea what this could mean, but I think Dante's men should look into it."

"We will," Dante assured them. "But back to my original point. Your sister knows how the system works, that if she destroyed Gonzalez's drugs, she'd be dead. So, when his lawyer talked to her in jail, I assure you the first thing she told him, regardless of how much she may love you, is that you're the one who flushed that cocaine. She probably told him you tricked her somehow into taking the drugs in the first place. Basically, she gave him what he wanted, a way to place blame on someone else and not hurt her. But by doing that, she moved you to the top of

Gonzalez's hit list. I imagine his lawyer was supposed to bail you out of jail so Gonzalez's men could abduct you. When that didn't work, he took Lily and tempted you to the Keys with that note. Going to Skeleton's Misery was like offering yourself up as a gift. The end result was inevitable, that Gonzalez would send someone to kill you. Lucky for you, Nick stepped in. Unfortunately for Nick, it cost him his job."

Heather froze, her heart stuttering in her chest. "I don't...I don't understand," she whispered. "Nick?"

His jaw tightened. "When Dante called Waverly to report what happened, Waverly fired me for not staying in Saint Augustine and for coming down here without permission."

Heather's stomach twisted into a hard knot. She knew Nick loved being a DEA agent. It seemed to matter more to him than anything else.

Including her.

If he hadn't hated her before, he must hate her now. "But you were a hero. You saved Mark and me."

"Exactly what I said to Waverly," Dante said. "If it weren't for Nick, Agent Watkins would be dead. Of that I have no doubt. And you would probably be in one of Gonzalez's compounds right now being interrogated by Gonzalez or one of his men. Nick saved both of you, several times from what I've heard. He's extremely good at what he does, which is why I offered him a position on my team. Unfortunately, he turned me down."

"What?" Heather grabbed Nick's hand. "Why would you do that? You shouldn't lose your job because of me."

He gently pulled his hand back. "For the same reason I defied Waverly by coming down here in the first place. I don't want you to get hurt. And now Dante wants to put you in danger just like Waverly. I'm not going to allow that. After this meeting, you and I are going back home, to Saint Augustine."

Panic bloomed inside Heather, making her legs shake. "I can't go back, not without Lily."

"I agree," Dante said. "And I have a plan to help get her back."

Nick swore, leaving Heather little doubt that he knew exactly what Dante's plan was.

And he didn't like it.

"Okay, what's the plan?" she asked.

Dante grinned. "We're going to play the identical twin card."

Chapter Nine

"You're proposing the same ill-fated plan Waverly proposed," Nick said, his voice low and menacing.

"Close, yes, but far less dangerous, because I'll make sure she's protected," Dante said. "Miss Bannon, believe me when I tell you I would never have agreed to Rickloff and Waverly's plan had they asked me ahead of time. But the wheels are in motion and two agents were nearly killed. That sends the wrong signal to the bad guys. If I don't bring Gonzalez down, I might as well declare open season on all my agents. To get him, I need inside information, which has proved exceedingly difficult with Gonzalez. His men are so afraid of him they're loyal without question." He leaned forward in his chair. "I'm proposing a twist in the original plan. Instead of presenting yourself as Heather, I want you to pretend to be Lily."

Heather blinked, not certain she'd heard him correctly. "Excuse me?"

Nick mumbled something that sounded like "stupid plan" and "dangerous" beneath his breath.

Heather clutched the arms of her chair in frustration. "If Gonzalez has my sister, how can I pretend to be her in public? Everyone will know I'm a fraud."

Dante shook his head. "Last night, no one thought you were Lily. You didn't dress like her or act like her, because you weren't trying to pretend to be her. Gonzalez had no problem sending men after you because you were obviously *not* your sister. But if you can convince everyone you're Lily, he has to be more careful. If his men grabbed Lily in public, he'd be sending the message his mistress had defied him, and he'd be forced to kill her. But he doesn't want to kill her. So, instead, he'll come after you himself and try to bargain with you so you'll go with him without making a fuss, allowing him to save face and not hurt his girlfriend."

Heather shook her head. "This is all so confusing. But I'll do whatever I can to save her. How will your plan do that?"

"After forcing Gonzalez out into the open, we'll be able to follow him back to see where he's holding your sister. Then we can get a warrant and raid the compound and free Lily. The beauty of it is that I then get to charge Gonzalez with kidnapping. I'll take that to get him off the streets. Of course, we'll have to figure out how to make all of this happen, without Gonzalez taking you prisoner as well."

Nick swore. "Yet another reason not to use her

in this crazy scheme. There's no way to guarantee her safety. Your plan isn't any better than Rickloff's or Waverly's."

Dante frowned at him. "Waverly sent a civilian with one agent and no backup. That was stupid. I'll send her in with plenty of backup. And we'll have every possible escape route covered."

Nick shook his head. "There has to be another way to find Gonzalez and rescue Lily without putting Heather in danger."

"We have no way of knowing where Gonzalez is holding Lily. We need a way to narrow it down. If you have a better plan, please, tell me. I'm listening." Dante leaned back in his chair and folded his hands behind his head.

"Send your men to all the local bars," Nick said. "Let them infiltrate Gonzalez's network and gather information, find out where he is. Use all this fancy equipment and resources you have to launch a rescue operation."

"That will take too long—weeks, months.

Even though Gonzalez has hidden Lily's thievery from most of his men, his close inner circle has to know what happened by now. He can't afford not to punish her. And he's not going to wait weeks or months."

The unspoken conclusion seemed to weigh on everyone in the room. Lily was still in danger, mortal danger.

Nick glared at Dante. "What, exactly, do you want Heather to do?"

"One of Gonzalez's men's favorite hangouts is a marina a couple of miles north of here. There's a restaurant on the boardwalk that's considerably more tame than Skeleton's Misery. We'll have men inside and out, and scattered throughout the marina. Heather will wear a wire and sit as bait, waiting for Gonzalez to approach. She'll walk outside with him and we'll cause some kind of commotion to let her escape. Then we'll follow Gonzalez without him realizing it."

"Won't he smell a trap?" Nick asked.

"Possibly. I didn't say the plan was perfect, just that I don't have a better one."

"I don't think he'll show," Nick insisted.

"You may be right," Dante said, his tone matter-of-fact as if that didn't really matter. "I'd give it fifty-fifty odds. But even if he doesn't show, having Miss Bannon pretend to be Lily will stir things up. That might increase the activity in the compound where Gonzalez is holding the real Lily. If Gonzalez thinks the DEA is going all out to trap him and find Lily, he may have his security doubled or tripled where he's holding her." He gestured toward the screen on the far wall. "We've got eyes on all of his major holdings. If he starts making changes, we'll know about it. Once we know where she's being held, we can do everything the old-fashioned way, get down to basics and perform twenty-four-hour surveillance until he makes a mistake. Then we'll get that warrant and go in."

Nick stared down at the floor for a moment.

Heather watched him carefully. She trusted his judgment. She wanted to save her sister, and she believed Nick was her best chance. If he didn't want her to go along with Dante's plan, she wouldn't. She'd learned her lesson. But if he did agree to the plan, she'd do whatever it took to help.

Nick looked up and met her gaze. "Do you want to do this?" he asked quietly.

"I want to save my sister. If you think this is our best shot, then yes, I want to do it. It's your decision."

His brows rose in surprise. He stared at her for a full minute before blowing out a breath and sitting back. "All right, Dante. Reinstate me and put me in charge. I plan every single detail down to which men come along, where they sit, even what weapons they have. The second I feel antsy, I pull Heather out. You either agree to my terms, or we're leaving."

Heather couldn't help but smile. Nick was all

about conditions, and he was reciting condition number two to Dante.

Dante slapped his hands on his thighs and grinned. "Agreed." He stood and held his hand out to Nick.

Nick rolled his eyes and stood to shake his hand. "You had this planned all along, didn't you?"

"You bet. Waverly's loss is my gain. Welcome to my team. When do you want the operation to take place?"

Nick looked at his watch. "Might as well do it tonight. We'll plan everything out right now. Then you can work on putting all the pieces in place while I take Heather back to Saint Augustine for a couple of hours."

Heather frowned. "Why would we go back home?"

"Because if you're going to pretend to be your sister, you've got to look like her. That means finding the perfect clothes, which my sister-in-law can help with. But more importantly, it means going where I have a special contact with very special skills."

Heather stared at him suspiciously. He looked like he was suddenly enjoying this way too much. "What special skills?"

He grinned. "Tattoos."

HEATHER BALKED AT the entrance to the tattoo parlor. The look of distaste on her face as she stared at the sign over the door was priceless. Nick knew he was having far too much fun teasing her, but he also knew she was far too uptight and nervous for tonight's dangerous operation. He needed her to loosen up, to have some fun, to relax. And if he enjoyed himself along the way, so be it.

She bit her lip. "Are you absolutely sure it won't hurt? And that the tattoos won't be permanent?"

Nick grinned. "Permanent wouldn't be so bad,

would it?" He leaned down next to her ear. "Show me yours and I'll show you mine."

She rolled her eyes.

Nick winked and pulled the door open, ushering her inside.

"I still don't see why we had to fly all the way to Saint Augustine for this," she grumbled.

"This is my home turf. I know whom to trust here. And we couldn't risk anyone in Key West finding out about you getting these fake tattoos. They have to believe the tattoos are real, that you're Lily, for this to work."

She stared up at him. "You were just teasing me about having a tattoo, right? I know you don't have any."

"You sure about that?" He dipped his head again, his mouth hovering next to her ear. "We only made love once. Are you sure you saw every...single...inch of me?"

Heather blinked, her face flushing an adorable shade of pink.

Nick laughed out loud, thoroughly enjoying himself.

"Can I help you folks?" A man shorter than Heather, with tattoos completely covering his arms from shoulder to wrist, stepped in from the back. When he saw Nick, he smiled and held out his hand.

"Hey, man, it's been a while. You here for a touch-up?"

Heather stared at Nick in surprise. He could practically see the thoughts whirling through her mind as she tried to figure out where his tattoo might be. She deliberately turned her back on him, pretending to study a book on the counter that contained dozens of designs.

"Nope, I'm not here for me today, Mitch. This is Heather, a friend of mine."

Heather turned around and shook his hand, but she didn't look at Nick.

"What can I do for y'all?" Mitch asked.

In answer, Nick pulled some copies of Lily's

mug shots out of his shirt pocket. He and Heather had stopped at the station earlier for the photos. They were the only pictures that clearly showed Lily's tattoos.

Mitch didn't even blink when Nick handed him the pictures. Apparently mug shots weren't anything new to him.

"I need you to reproduce these tattoos on Heather. I need them to look exactly like the pictures, but they need to be temporary, lasting no more than a couple of weeks."

"Afraid to commit, huh?" He smiled at Heather. "Don't worry, you'll fall in love with my artwork. I guarantee you'll be back once this starts to fade. You'll want me to make everything permanent."

"Don't count on it." She allowed him to lead her to a chair that resembled the kind in dentist offices.

The bell above the door rang. Nick turned and

smiled with genuine pleasure. He stepped over to greet his brother and sister-in-law.

HEATHER TRIED NOT to be too obvious with her interest as she watched Rafe Morgan enter the shop. She'd only met him once, after she'd called 911 about her sister's abduction and he escorted her to the police station. She'd never understood why he'd been the first to arrive after her 911 call, since he was a detective and not a uniformed officer. But he must have been close by and responded when the call came in.

She hadn't really noticed much about him at the time because she was so focused on her sister's disappearance. But now, seeing him standing with Nick, she was struck by how alike they were in height and build, but how very different they were in other ways. Rafe had dark hair and dark eyes. He didn't smile nearly as much as his blond brother, or laugh the way Nick tended to do. Rafe was definitely the more serious of the two.

"Heather?" A soft voice had Heather turning around. She'd been so busy staring at Nick and his brother that she hadn't realized the petite woman who'd come inside with Rafe was now standing beside her chair. Mitch was a few feet away, in his own little world, studying the pictures of the tattoos as if he were Michelangelo preparing to paint the Sistine Chapel.

"You must be Nick's sister-in-law," Heather said, offering her hand and a smile.

The woman shook Heather's hand and returned her smile. She pushed a thick strand of dark hair back from her face. Her chic-looking bob swished back and forth every time she moved. Her suit was perfectly tailored to fit her tiny figure, and looked like it cost more than Heather could earn on a month of stakeouts.

"Yes, I'm Darby. Mind if I sit down?"

Heather shook her head, and Darby pulled a

folding chair from nearby and sat. "Nick called Rafe earlier this morning and asked if I could pick up some clothes for you. He said you might have some pictures I could use to get some outfits for the case you're working on. I'd love to help. I know all the specialty shops around here. I can find whatever you need and make it back before Mitch is finished."

Heather shot a glance at Nick. He was still talking to his brother, but he was watching her.

"Um, what exactly did Nick tell you about me?"

"All he said was that you were going undercover on a case together." She hesitated, glancing at Nick before continuing. "But I know Nick fairly well," she said, lowering her voice. "I can tell he cares about you. I've never seen him so… focused on anyone. I know you two have some sort of past, but Rafe wouldn't give me any details." She grinned. "Even though I tried everything I could to get him to tell me, after Nick called this morning."

Heather sighed. "I wish you were right about Nick, but I'm afraid if he's focused it's because he doesn't trust me. Let's just say, he's judged me and found me lacking."

Darby frowned. "Hmm. Maybe you're right. I could have sworn…well, it doesn't matter. How about it? Are you going to let me pick out some clothes for you?"

Mitch laid out his tools on a tray beside the chair and waited expectantly. He was obviously ready to get on with his plans to pepper Heather's arms and torso with tattoos.

Heather grimaced and leaned in close to Darby. "Thank goodness he's not going to give me any real tattoos. I can't imagine having someone stick me with needles and paint my skin permanently."

Darby's eyes sparkled with mischief. "It's not

as bad as you think. And the right tattoo, in the right location, can drive a man crazy."

Heather laughed, surprised a woman as conservative-looking as Darby might actually have a tattoo. "Are you saying that you—"

Darby nodded, her face flushing a light pink. "Now give me those pictures so I can go shopping. By the time I'm done, you won't recognize yourself."

Heather gave her a wan smile. As she passed copies of Lily's pictures to Darby, she felt her face flush warm. She wished she had other pictures of her sister, but these were the only ones. She and Lily didn't exactly go for photo ops when Lily blew into town.

Darby's eyes widened. "Are these—"

"Mug shots. Yes. That's my twin sister. Is that a problem?"

Darby cleared her throat and shoved the pictures into her purse. "Of course not. Just leave everything to me."

Chapter Ten

Leaving everything to Darby had been a colossal mistake.

Back at the hotel in Key West again, Heather desperately searched her suitcase one more time and shook her head in disbelief. Darby had taken her shopping assignment to the extreme. She'd bought three outfits, probably to give Heather a choice. But every single one was far too risqué. Even the underwear was like what her sister would wear. The bras were tiny scraps of lace that would barely support her. The panties looked like neon silly string. There was no way Heather could wear this stuff.

She wanted to make others believe she was Lily, yes, but she couldn't dress quite as…revealing as her sister did. She'd mentioned that to Darby. She was sure of it, and yet everything Darby had bought was too short or too tight or just plain too indecent for Heather to even consider wearing.

She sighed and flipped the suitcase closed. Instead, she pulled some of her own clothes out of the closet. She mixed and matched, trying to figure out something that would work. The above-the-knee skirt and short-sleeved blouse would have to do. Mitch's amazing artwork would show just fine with this top. That's all that mattered.

Nick was sitting at the small table next to the kitchenette studying a map spread out before him when she walked out of the bedroom.

His brows climbed to his hairline and he rolled his eyes. "Please tell me that's not what

Darby bought you. Didn't you give her the pictures of Lily?"

Heather glanced down at her ensemble. It's not like she'd tucked the blouse in or anything. She'd left the last three buttons undone and had even dared to tie the ends of the blouse together. For goodness' sake, her belly button was showing. No one who knew her would ever expect her to dress like this, not even on one of her forays into the bar scene while doing her P.I. job.

"The clothes Darby bought didn't work out, so I had to get creative with some of my old clothes." She waved her hand at her blouse. "This is like something Lily would wear."

Nick laughed. "No. It isn't." He pushed back from his chair and strode toward her.

"How would you know? You only met her once. The night you threw both of us in jail."

He stopped in front of her. "We're not having that argument tonight. We have too much to do."

She crossed her arms over her chest. "Have

you even seen the cell where they house the women prisoners? It's disgusting. It smells like pee."

His lips twitched. Lucky for him, he didn't smile, or she would have been tempted to kick him in the groin.

"No, I didn't know it smelled like…pee," he said. He grabbed her hand and pulled her toward the bedroom.

"What are you doing? I thought you wanted to get to the bar by nine."

"You're not going out looking like that. No one would believe you were Lily." He let her hand go and flipped the suitcase open on top of the bed. He pulled out a pink tank top with spaghetti straps. "How about this?"

She shook her head and held the top against her. "Look how short it is. It would barely cover my breasts."

He stared at the shirt for a moment. He swallowed hard and cleared his throat. "Right." He grabbed another shirt out of the suitcase and held it up.

Heather shook her head. "Too low-cut. I'd fall out."

Nick's gaze shot to her chest, as if he were trying to imagine just that thing. His mouth tightened and he balled up the shirt and tossed it onto the bed. He dug around in the suitcase some more. "Aha." He pulled out a leopard-print tank and held it up. "Long enough to, ah, cover you and not too low-cut."

She took the shirt and held it up, eyeing it critically. "There's something that isn't quite right about this." She understood the spaghetti strap on the right side. But what held it up on the left side? The neckline didn't even look straight. She was seriously having doubts about Darby's so-called shopping expertise. "I'm not even sure I know how to put this on."

Nick pulled a short black miniskirt out of the suitcase and handed it to her. "You'll figure it out. Hurry. We should have left ten minutes ago."

She huffed and headed into the bathroom to change. A few minutes later, she stared at herself in the mirror, horrified.

A knock sounded on the door. "I've got your shoes. Or, at least, I think these are the right shoes. They're black. That matches everything, right?"

"I am not wearing this…this…outfit," Heather said, raising her voice so he could hear her. "I look like a hooker."

The door opened. Heather's gaze shot to Nick's in the mirror as he stepped in behind her. He set a pair of six-inch stilettos on the countertop.

Heather gasped. "I can't possibly wear those… those medieval foot-torturing devices. I'd break my neck."

He grinned. "Medieval torture, huh?" He cocked his head to the side, studying her reflection. "I don't think that's the way that's supposed to work." He tugged the left side of the shirt off her shoulder. "There. That looks better."

Heather stared into the mirror. One side of the shirt was held up by the spaghetti strap. The other side hung low, revealing far more of her breasts than she'd ever revealed in public before, except maybe at the beach in a swimsuit. Even then, she wasn't sure she'd shown off this much skin. She shook her head. "I can't do it. I can't go out like this. The top is—"

"Perfect. It shows off your lovely…tattoos." His grin broadened, letting her know he'd substituted tattoos at the last second.

She eyed the artwork Mitch had so painstakingly painted on her arms and upper body. The pink dragon peeked out of the top of her skirt. She'd blushed profusely the entire time Mitch was working on that particular tattoo. Her skin had felt as though it was on fire, especially when

Nick sat down beside her, watching every stroke, after Rafe and Darby left on the shopping trip.

"That one's my favorite," Nick breathed next to her ear.

She shivered and refused to meet his gaze.

He picked up the shoes and held them out. "I can't wait to see how you look in these." The teasing laughter in his voice told her he knew how hard it was for her to stand here in this outfit, and he was having fun at her expense.

"No," she said. "I told you I'm not wearing those. And I'm not wearing this ridiculous outfit. I'll put my own clothes back on." She turned to leave, but he didn't budge an inch.

His thighs pressed up against hers and his chest rubbed against her breasts. He set the shoes on the countertop and braced his hands on the sink, trapping her.

"How did you and your sister grow up in the same household and end up so completely different?" His voice was low and husky. There was no mistaking the heat in his gaze, or the way his pulse was slamming in his chest. She could feel every beat of his heart against hers.

"Let me guess. You prefer the way my sister dresses."

"I didn't say that. But dressing so…minimally…does have its advantages." He winked.

Heather didn't know what to make of his flirty mood. She tried to focus on her memories of the jail cell to combat her softening feelings toward a man she could never have, but with Nick standing so close, all she could think of was how good his hard body felt against her soft curves. And how perfectly…edible he smelled.

He reached up and traced the barbed-wire tattoo on her left bicep. "So, how did two identical twin sisters end up so different?"

Heather cleared her throat and took a step back to put some space between them. "Lily was always, ah, competitive, jealous, I guess. She thought I was the favorite. And she…" She shivered when Nick smoothed his fingers up her other arm, lightly tracing the outline of one of the swirling flower tattoos.

"And she…what?" He slid his hand up her shoulder.

"She left home when she was sixteen. Dropped out of school. I didn't see her for a long time. I only recently…"

He gently massaged her shoulder, making her skin flush hot wherever he touched her.

"Go on," he urged, both of his hands heating her skin, leaving a fiery trail in their wake. "You recently what?"

"I…I don't remember what I was going to say. Nick, what are you doing?"

His nostrils flared and he dipped his head down toward her, but before his mouth claimed hers, he hesitated. Time seemed to stand still as Heather looked into his eyes, so close to hers.

"Nick?" she breathed, waiting, hoping.

He shuddered, his brow furrowing as if he

were in pain. Then he stepped back and turned away. "I'll wait in the living room. Don't change clothes. What you're wearing is perfect for pretending to be your sister. If you want to get Gonzalez to notice you, that's the way to do it."

His voice was hard and cold, with none of the warmth she'd heard earlier. He stalked from the bathroom, leaving her wondering what in the world had just happened.

"DON'T FORGET CONDITION number two," Nick said.

Heather clutched his hand, afraid she wasn't going to be able to do this. He had her backed up against the wall in the dark hallway to the bathrooms in the marina restaurant, pretending to be amorous in case someone saw them, but he was actually giving her last-minute instructions.

"Heather, did you hear what I said?"

"Condition number two, yes, got it." She glanced down the long hall toward the main room of the restaurant. She had to go out there, by herself, in this horrid outfit, and pretend to be okay with that while she waited for a dangerous drug dealer to approach her. She clutched Nick's hand even harder.

He cursed and gently eased her grip, bringing her attention back to him.

"Sorry," she whispered.

"It's okay. What's condition number two?" he asked. "I need to make sure you've got this."

"I hate your stupid conditions."

"I know, but tell me anyway."

She rolled her eyes. "Condition number two—I do exactly what you tell me to do at all times. I remember. And don't worry. I've got that ear thingy in. I'm not going to try to wing it on my own. I'm scared enough as it is."

His mouth twitched. "Earwig, not ear thingy. And why are you scared? It's just a restaurant, nothing like the bar you were in before. There are no fewer than ten DEA agents in here undercover, plus me. You're surrounded by people who want nothing more than to keep you safe. Nothing's going to happen, as long as you follow instructions. The second I feel it's not safe, I'm pulling you out. If I tell you to leave, you jump out of your chair and hightail it out of here. Some of the agents will follow you out. If I tell you to duck down, you—"

"Yeah, yeah. I drop to the floor. You reminded me of all your conditions a million times on the way over here. I've got it. And I've got *this*. I didn't dress up like a two-bit hooker for nothing. I'm not going to humiliate myself looking like this without doing everything I can to make this work. I don't want to have to come back here again. I want this to end tonight."

His hand circled her waist and he pulled her close. "Trust me. You don't look like a two-bit hooker."

"I don't?" she whispered, her breath catching in her throat at the heat in his gaze.

He shook his head. "I'd pay a lot more than two bits." He winked.

She drew a sharp breath and shoved his hand away. Without another word, she whirled around and headed for the high-topped table reserved for her. Her dramatic exit was ruined when she lost her balance on the ridiculous stilettos and almost fell. She grabbed the back of a chair, forcing a smile when the startled man in the chair turned.

With a slower, more sane pace, she made her way to the table. She climbed onto the bar stool, certain she looked like a fool trying to keep from flashing everyone as she tugged on her miniskirt.

When a waitress stopped by, Heather ordered her sister's favorite drink, tequila, straight up. But when the drink arrived, Heather only pretended to sip it. The smell alone told her she'd be gagging or half drunk in minutes if she really drank any.

It didn't take long for someone to notice her. A tall, thin man with coffee-colored skin threaded his way through the crowd to her table. She could see him out of the corner of her eye, but she focused instead on watching the people at the other tables, eating dinner.

"Stranger approaching at two o'clock. He's not Gonzalez, but he might be one of his men," Nick's voice spoke in her ear through the two-way transmitter. Heather couldn't help but jump when his voice first sounded. Hopefully no one noticed.

"Mmm-hmm." She raised her glass for a pretend sip.

"Lily." The man she'd seen approaching was suddenly standing beside her chair. "What are you doing here?" He glanced around, as if afraid someone might see him with her.

Her pulse sped up. This man obviously knew her sister, and expected she would know him, too. She tried to focus on what Nick had told her to do. Lowering her glass, she crossed her arms on the table and tried for a world-weary expression.

"What do you think I'm doing? I'm having a drink."

He leaned in close, still not looking at her directly. He kept scanning the room as if he was afraid someone was watching him. "Obviously, but why here?"

"Why not here?" she countered. "Where else should I be?"

He quirked a brow, facing her directly this time. "Does Gonzalez know you left the compound?"

"Be evasive," Nick's voice whispered through the transmitter in her ear.

Heather moved her glass in tiny circles on the tabletop. "I couldn't say if he knows or not. He doesn't own me. He doesn't tell me what I can or can't do."

The man's brows lifted. "How much have you been drinking?"

"Not enough." She lifted the glass and held it to her lips. Then she set it back down and wiped her mouth. "Say whatever it is you want to say and go away. You're ruining my good mood."

He shook his head, his face reddening. "If Gonzalez realizes you left, there won't be a safe place within hundreds of miles for you to hide. You'd better go back, now, before he realizes you're gone."

"Go back where?" She purposely slurred her words, trying to give him the impression she was a little tipsy, to explain why she wouldn't know where Gonzalez was.

He shook his head. "Come on. I'll take you back."

Excitement pulsed through her. Could it really be this easy? He was offering to take her to where Gonzalez was holding her sister. She took a slow, deep breath, trying to remain calm.

"All right, I guess. This place is boring anyway. You'll have to drive though. This tequila's already gone straight to my head."

He gave her a quizzical look. "Drive?"

Shoot. What had she done? She was being too specific, which could ruin everything since she didn't have a clue where Gonzalez's compound was. Why would he balk at the word *drive?* Was the compound so close they could walk there? Or was it so far away they would have to fly, or take a boat? She wasn't sure what to say.

The transmitter crackled in her ear. "Play up how much you drank. He's getting suspicious."

She grinned and lifted her drink again. "What? You don't think I could do it? Drive to the compound?" She giggled, trying to make him think she thought the idea was ridiculous, too.

"You really are wasted." He pulled the drink away from her and shoved it out of her reach. "Come on. My boat's out back. I'll try to sneak you into the compound before all hell breaks loose."

"Okay, walk outside with him but stay close to the restaurant," Nick's voice whispered in her ear. "Try to get him to tell you where the compound is. If he doesn't, ditch him and go back inside to wait for Gonzalez."

She slid off the bar stool. She immediately had to clutch the table for support when her feet wobbled in her outrageously unstable stilettos.

The man with her cursed and grabbed her arm, steadying her. He obviously thought she was too drunk to walk, because he held her close and guided her out of the bar.

"We're with you," Nick's voice whispered. "But you're too close to him. Put some distance between the two of you. And under no circumstances are you to get anywhere near his boat. Make an excuse. Say you have to go to the bathroom, whatever it takes. We'll follow his boat when he leaves and see where he goes. With any luck, that will give us the location of the compound where Lily is. Now back away. You're still too close."

With any luck? Meaning if she didn't get on the boat, this might all be for nothing and they might not find Lily? Heather frowned, but did as Nick had told her. She pulled away from the man beside her.

"I can walk," she said, slurring her words again. "Just lead the way. Um, where are we going again?" She threw the last part in, hoping he'd say the name of the island where the compound was, if indeed it was on another island, which she assumed because of him saying they would take his boat to get there.

"To the compound," he said.

Her hopes plummeted as the boats sitting at the dock came into view. If she couldn't get him to give her the location, she'd gained nothing. What if they lost him once he took the boat out?

What if Gonzalez didn't show, and this was her only shot?

"I know, I know," she said, forcing another giggle. "But where is that again? I can't seem to keep it straight in my head." She tapped her temple and wobbled on her heels, this time on purpose.

He ignored her question.

"Go back to the restaurant," Nick hissed in her ear.

Heather kept walking.

When they reached the stranger's boat, he held out his hand to help her. "Come on."

She should have backed away. She should have told him she had to go to the ladies' room as Nick had suggested. But she hesitated. This man knew where Lily was.

"Why are you still standing there?" Nick whispered. "Go back inside the restaurant."

"Hurry up," the stranger said, waving his hand for her to step over the side of the boat. "I'm telling you, if Gonzalez figures out you managed to leave without him knowing, it's not just you who's in trouble. It's me and the other guys who are supposed to be guarding the place."

"Don't you dare," Nick's furious voice whispered in her ear, as if he'd just realized she was seriously considering getting into the boat. "Get out of there," he demanded.

She glanced down at the man's hand in front of her. If she stepped into that boat, she'd see her sister again. Or would she? What if this was a trick? But if she didn't, she was back at the beginning, no closer to finding her twin than she'd been on day one. How much more time did Lily have if she wasn't rescued? A week? A day? An hour?

"Heather." Nick's voice was a low growl. "Condition number two."

She stiffened her spine. "I'm sorry," she whispered. "I have to do this."

"What?" The man's brows lowered in confusion.

"Nothing." She smiled and took his hand.

Nick cursed in her ear. He sounded out of breath, as if he was on the move.

Heather stepped over the side of the boat, and all hell broke loose.

Chapter Eleven

The hand holding Heather's went slack. The man in front of her crumpled to the floor of the boat. Behind him stood the man Dante had shown her a picture of earlier, to make sure she'd recognize him.

Gonzalez.

In his hand was the gun he'd used like a hammer to knock the other man unconscious.

Heather stood frozen, staring into the eyes of the man who'd taken her sister. Gonzalez started to raise his gun. A man suddenly lunged from the shadows beside the boat and launched himself at Gonzalez, slamming into him, propelling both of them over the side and into the water. The splash sent up a plume of water that would have drenched Heather if someone hadn't grabbed her and pulled her back.

Like ants pouring out of an anthill, a dozen DEA agents converged onto the docks from their hiding places behind bushes, boats and even the cars parked near the dock. Two agents standing at the water's edge discarded their jackets and guns and jumped into the water where Gonzalez and the other man had disappeared.

"Miss Bannon, this way, please." The man who'd pulled Heather out of the boat tugged her backward. The big white *DEA* letters on his jacket reassured Heather that he really was an agent and wasn't one of Gonzalez's men, but the fact that he wasn't Nick had her stomach clenching with dread. Where was Nick? Had something happened to him? She replayed the last few moments in her memory.

The man who'd taken her to the boat crumpling to the floor.

Gonzalez standing behind him with a gun in his hand.

Another man launching himself at Gonzalez.

A very familiar-looking man.

Heather's gaze flew back to the boat and the crowd of men standing there.

"Please tell me that wasn't Agent Nick Morgan who went into the water with Gonzalez."

"Well, yes, ma'am, it was."

She tugged out of the man's grasp and ran toward the water's edge. Or at least, that was her plan. She'd only gone about five feet when her right heel wobbled, she lost her balance and she went sprawling onto the asphalt.

Her mind had just enough time to register that her miniskirt was hiked up around her hips before someone hauled her to her feet and tugged her skirt back into place. From the sounds of the cursing in her ear, she knew exactly who'd come to her rescue this time.

Nick.

She was so relieved that he was okay that she didn't even care that he was yelling at her in front of everyone for being so stupid and fool-ishly risking her life. And she didn't care that he was dripping wet. All she cared about was that he wasn't dead.

She threw her arms around his waist and held him tight. "Thank God you're okay."

He stiffened and grabbed her arms, forcing her back. He grabbed one of the agents nearby. "Higgins, get Miss Bannon back to the hotel. Take another agent with you and try to keep her from causing any more trouble until I get back."

"Yes, sir." Higgins motioned another agent over. "Miss Bannon, come with us, please."

Without another word, Nick stalked off and joined the group of men surrounding a very wet, very angry-looking Gonzalez, who'd been fished out of the water.

Heather wanted to jump into the water herself, or maybe throw one of those DEA flak jackets over her head, anything to shut herself away from the other agents giving her curious looks. They'd seen her hugging Nick. And they'd seen him push her away. He'd treated her like a stranger and spoke to her as if she were a recalcitrant child. Perhaps if she were a child, or a stranger, he'd at least have asked if she was okay. Instead, he'd been too busy putting as much distance between them as he could, as quickly as he could.

As if she didn't even matter.

"Miss Bannon?" Higgins gave her a quizzical look. "Are you okay?"

His kind question and gentle voice had her tearing up. Why couldn't Nick have shown some compassion, an ounce of caring, instead of being so disgusted with her? She didn't have cocaine in her hair this time, but he'd still treated her as if she had the plague.

In front of everyone.

She gave Higgins a tight smile. "I'm fine. I'm ready to go. Thank you."

He nodded and led her toward a waiting car. She kept her head up, her back straight, refusing to let Nick have the satisfaction of thinking his treatment of her mattered. It was all her fault, really. She'd forgotten about condition number one. The words Nick had said to her at the police station couldn't have been more clear when he'd listed his first condition for agreeing to help her.

We're through, finished. There is no "us" anymore. And there never will be.

She'd been in total agreement at the time, right after she'd gotten out of jail. She'd wanted nothing to do with him, either. But just being near him the past few days had reminded her how much she was attracted to him, how much she admired him for the work he did, how much he cared about helping other people. Seeing the lighter side of him with his brother and sister-in-law at the tattoo parlor had reminded her how warm and loving he could be, a side of him she'd enjoyed so much when they first met, but which she'd seen so little of in the past few days.

How could she have allowed herself to fall for him again only to be rejected again? He didn't want her. He didn't care about her. All he cared about was his job and appearances.

She wouldn't forget again.

THE SOUND OF voices woke Heather. She bolted up in bed, blinking to focus in the dimly lit hotel room as she clutched the covers to her chest. Her pulse was pounding so hard she could hear it echoing in her ears.

The low murmur of a deep male voice sounded again, and Heather slumped with relief. Nick. He was in the main room of their hotel suite, talking to the two agents guarding her. A few moments later, she heard the sound of a door closing. The other agents must have left.

She glanced at the bedside clock. Two in the morning. Good grief. What had Nick been doing out this late? Had he helped interview Gonzalez? That thought had her fully awake. If he'd spoken to Gonzalez, he might know where her sister was. The DEA could be on their way right now to rescue her. She fervently hoped so.

She shoved the covers back and hopped out of bed right as her bedroom door flew open. She gasped and pressed her hand to her throat before her mind registered that it was Nick standing in the doorway.

She drew in a shaky breath. "You scared me." She lowered her hand to her side, grateful the only light in the room was from the moonlight filtering in through the blinds. She was only wearing a T-shirt and panties, and after Nick's treatment of her back at the dock had reminded her about condition number one, she wasn't exactly comfortable parading around in her underwear.

"Did you find out anything from Gonzalez? Do you know where my sister is?" She reached for the light blanket at the foot of the bed to wrap around herself.

Nick stalked toward the bed, stopping just short of touching her. The tightness of his jaw and the way his eyes narrowed dangerously had Heather's survival instincts screaming at her to run. She resisted the cowardly urge because she knew Nick would never hurt her—not physically, anyway—and her pride had taken too much of a beating already tonight. She wasn't about to let him bully her.

He leaned down toward her, obviously trying to use his size and strength to intimidate her.

It was working.

"What were you thinking?" he bit out, his voice a tight rasp. He grabbed her arms and lightly shook her. "What were you thinking when you stepped onto that boat?"

His shaking her and talking to her in that condescending, sarcastic tone was the proverbial last straw. She was through with his conditions, through with him bullying her, through with him ordering her around. She picked up her feet and dropped right out of his arms. She twisted and threw all her weight at the back of his knees.

He crashed to the floor like a rock.

Heather crouched beside him, ready to lecture him on manners, but the sight of big, tough Nick lying flat on his back, blinking up at her with such a look of astonishment on his face, tugged at her funny bone. A giggle burst between her lips.

Nick's eyes narrowed in warning.

Another giggle escaped. Heather clasped her hand over her mouth, but it was hopeless. She started laughing so hard tears streamed down her face.

"Oh, oh, my gosh." She wiped her tears. "The look on your face when you…" She laughed again, so hard her stomach hurt. She clutched at her middle, drawing big gasping breaths between laughs.

Nick grabbed her and suddenly *she* was the one flat on her back. He covered her body with his. "Stop laughing," he growled.

"I'm…trying," she wheezed between giggles. The memory of his shocked look triggered another round of laughter.

Suddenly his mouth was on hers. The crazy man must have thought he could stop her laughter by kissing her.

He was right.

The feel of his lips molding hers stopped her midgiggle, and suddenly all she wanted to do was kiss him back. She poured every ounce of frustration, hunger, even anger into that kiss. She wanted him, desperately, had wanted him for so long. And even though she knew it was probably a mistake, that she'd hate herself for it later, she wrapped her arms around his neck and pulled him closer, letting him know in every way she could that she wanted this.

He responded to her surrender like a starving man at a banquet. He peppered her with kisses, ran his tongue across her skin, suckled her until she cried out with pleasure. In a whisper of cloth her shirt was gone. A quick tug and her panties disappeared, too. Nick pushed himself off her for the briefest of moments as he tugged off his clothes. And then he was back, his naked skin heating hers, the light matting of hair on his chest scraping across her breasts, his arousal prodding her belly.

She shivered with wanting, longing for him to hurry and make her his. She couldn't bear the pleasure-pain of his wandering hands and sweltering kisses much longer.

"Nick, please..." she breathed against his neck.

Her urgency was matched by his. He pressed

another quick kiss against her lips, then pulled back.

"Give me a minute. I'll be right back."

Suddenly, he was gone, leaving her lying there, wondering why he'd run out of the room. But then he was back, and at the sound of a foil packet tearing open, her face turned warm. He was putting on a condom.

And then he was lifting and carrying her to the bed. He pushed her back against the mattress, doing sinful things to her neck, making her want him even more than she ever thought possible.

He suddenly grabbed her hips and pushed himself inside her in a long, deep stroke.

She cried out from the pleasure washing through her. Nick rasped her name and began to move again, building the tension inside her, higher and higher. He praised her, telling her how beautiful she was, how much he wanted her, as he stretched and filled her, bringing her closer and closer to the peak.

When she thought she was about to explode from the pleasure, he slowed his strokes and leaned down and kissed her again. He feathered his hands across her hypersensitive skin, learning every curve. Whenever he found a particularly sensitive spot, and her breath caught, he would pause and lavish her with more attention, as if to wring out every ounce of pleasure he could.

He shuddered, and Heather knew he was close. He kissed her again, then reached down between them, stroking her with his fingers as he thrust harder and faster into her. Heather drew her knees up, shouting his name as her climax washed over her, exploding through her body in a wave of pleasure so intense tears ran down her face.

Nick pushed fully into her, filling her, saying her name as he stiffened against her in his own climax. He shuddered again, collapsing on top of her for the barest of moments, then rolling to the side with her clasped tightly in his arms, as if reluctant to let her go.

As they lay together on the bed, their chests heaving from exertion, his hands stroking her bare back, she realized she'd never felt so complete as when she was in his arms. He couldn't have made love to her the way he had if he didn't care about her. He'd only yelled at her on the docks because he was worried about her. She knew that now.

She fell asleep with a smile on her face.

HEATHER'S DEEP, EVEN breathing told Nick she'd fallen asleep.

He continued to hold her and stroke the velvet-soft skin on her back. As his own skin cooled and the blood began pumping to his brain again, he realized what a terrible mistake he'd just made, in so many ways.

When he'd opened the door to her room, he hadn't meant to go on the offensive. He'd planned their conversation on the drive back from DEA headquarters. He was going to sit her down and calmly remind her how danger-ous this mission was. He was going to remind her they'd had to be extra careful because her barely there outfit wouldn't allow her to wear a bullet-resistant vest. He was going to remind her how crucial condition two was, that he'd set that condition out of concern for her safety, not because he wanted to boss her around.

But then he'd stepped into their hotel suite and had relived every agonizing moment of the encounter with Gonzalez as he briefed the two agents protecting Heather. He was furious with himself for agreeing to a plan that had put her in danger. A week ago, he wouldn't have even considered it. But after being with Heather these past few days, after seeing how deeply she cared about her sister, he'd realized she would be devastated if Lily died, and she'd never forgive him if he hadn't done everything he could to save her. He'd selfishly allowed his emotions to rule his head and had gone along with a far too dangerous plan.

Remembering Heather's blatant disregard for her own safety, how she'd been only a few feet from that sick, twisted psychopath, how he'd had a gun in his hand and could have easily killed her, all of that had his nerves stretched taut. When the agents stepped out of the suite, he'd been on the edge of desperation to assure himself that Heather was okay. He'd run to her room and had thrown the door open.

Her scantily clad body had been bathed in moonlight, her breasts pressing against her threadbare T-shirt, the lacy edge of her panties peeking at him beneath the hem. All the blood had pumped from his brain to another part of his anatomy. He wanted her, badly, wanted to feel her silky skin rubbing against his, hear her sexy little cries in the back of her throat when he plunged inside her. Wanting her, knowing he couldn't have her, had him clenching his jaw so tight his teeth ached.

So instead of holding her against him, he'd held her at arm's length, and his frustration that he couldn't do more than that had him saying things he shouldn't have said. Then she'd dropped him on his butt and started laughing, and all he could think about again was how much he wanted to kiss her. Just once, he'd told himself. One kiss, then he'd leave. But one kiss hadn't been enough, could never be enough.

He let out a deep sigh. The smile that was still on Heather's face, even in sleep, told him far more than she realized. That smile and the gift of her body tonight told him she'd forgiven him for arresting her and for abandoning her in that cell when he could have easily gotten her out.

But he didn't deserve her forgiveness, and he shouldn't have made love to her, because there was no turning back. There was no future for them. There was no way to pretend she'd never been arrested, that she hadn't broken the law to try to save her sister from going to jail—not without giving up his career. For him, being a DEA agent wasn't just a job. It was his life. It was who he was. He couldn't give that up, not if he had a choice.

He tucked the covers around her, then picked his clothes up off the floor and quietly walked to the door.

"Nick?"

He turned at the sound of her sleepy voice. "Yes?"

She propped herself up on her elbows. "You're leaving?"

He cleared his throat. "I'm going to my room. We both have to get up in just a few hours. We should get some sleep."

Even in the near-darkness he could tell she was weighing his words, searching for the truth hidden in them. He owed her the truth, and the sooner she knew it, the sooner they could both focus on the case again. And somehow find a way to move on.

He drew a deep, bracing breath.

"Don't say it." Heather's voice was frosty. "You don't have to say anything about…us." She laughed bitterly. "Condition number one, right?"

He briefly closed his eyes, hating the sound of hurt in her voice. "I'm sorry. It's not that I don't care about you. I—"

"Oh, please. Spare me, okay? I wanted you. I knew it was a mistake, that nothing had changed. My bad. What's done is done. Just tell me what happened with Gonzalez. Did you interview him? Did you find out where my sister is?"

He hesitated, feeling awkward, despising himself for hurting her. He also wasn't sure what to tell her. She'd find everything out in the morning, but if he told her what he'd learned, she wouldn't get any sleep, and she'd make herself sick with worry.

"Nick? You know something. Tell me." Her brows were drawn down and she was clutching the covers like a lifeline.

He sighed and chose a half truth. "Gonzalez didn't tell us where Lily's being held."

She closed her eyes briefly, as if she was in pain. "But did he at least tell you she's okay?"

"We don't know yet."

"But—"

"I'm sorry. There's nothing else I can tell you right now." Coming in here had been a mistake, one that he sorely regretted. He opened the door.

"Because you *can't* tell me, or because you won't?"

He answered without turning around. "Does it matter?"

"Yes."

"Because I can't. I honestly don't know if Lily is okay or not."

But he had every reason to believe she wasn't.

The silence stretched out between them. He finally turned around to look at her. She stared at him, as if she was deciding whether or not she could believe him.

"Thank you," she finally said, her voice firm, cold. "Thank you for telling me the truth."

He curled his fingers into his palms. He gave her a curt nod and stepped out of the room.

Chapter Twelve

For reasons Heather would understand all too soon, the DEA had taken Gonzalez to a secret location an hour north of Key West. Nick sat in the conference room beside Heather, waiting for Gonzalez to be brought in.

Heather was pale this morning, with dark circles under her eyes. She'd barely eaten anything for breakfast, no matter how much Nick cajoled and tried to talk her into taking care of herself. Knowing this was his fault had guilt eating him up inside.

Unfortunately, once she heard what Gonzalez

had to say, she was probably going to go from bad to worse.

Part of what Nick couldn't tell her last night was that he'd spent several hours at the docks, creating a cover story for what had happened. It was imperative that Gonzalez's capture be kept secret. But there had been several people who'd seen the swarm of DEA agents converging on that boat. Those people would see a story in the paper this morning that Nick had helped plant, a story that described a fiasco, painting the DEA as having mistakenly targeted a local fisherman thinking he was dealing drugs. But they'd found nothing. Their tip had turned out to be wrong, and there were no arrests to report.

The story would make it look like the DEA had bungled an investigation, a small price to pay for the agency to cover up what had really happened and to keep their original mission intact. Or at least, partly intact.

The true story from last night had changed everything.

"Are you sure you want to do this?" Nick asked. "You don't have to meet with him."

"I have to find my sister." She swallowed hard. "Or at least find out what happened to her. I'll talk to him. Did he…did he say why he wanted to talk to me? I mean, he knows I'm not Lily. So why would he insist on seeing me?"

Nick knew exactly why Gonzalez wanted to speak to her. Originally he'd thought it was kinder not to tell her ahead of time, because it would just drive her crazy hearing it from him, then having to make the long drive to speak to Gonzalez and ask the questions that would be going through her mind. Now Nick was second-guessing that decision. Maybe he should try to soften the blow by telling her himself, now, before Gonzalez came in.

"Look," he said, turning in his chair to face her. "I couldn't tell you this last night, but you're going to find out in a few minutes so I'm going to go ahead and tell you. When we brought Gonzalez in, he insisted that he wasn't—"

A knock sounded on the door. Before Nick could tell the agent on the other side to wait, the door opened. Two DEA agents came inside, flanking Gonzalez, who had chains dangling from his wrists and legs as he shuffled into the room.

Heather's complexion turned ashen. Regret curled inside Nick. He definitely should have warned her before they got here. She was in for a shock, and she was already shaking and looking impossibly frail. But there was no going back now.

Gonzalez's dark brown eyes went straight to Heather and never wavered, even as the agents wove chains from his cuffs to two shiny new steel hooks that had been bolted to the top of the table this morning for this very purpose. That was one of several things Nick had insisted on before allowing Heather anywhere near the man.

Another thing he'd insisted on was that Heather wasn't going to meet with Gonzalez alone. Gonzalez had been adamant, wanting to talk to her by himself. But Nick had refused to budge an inch, even when Dante had ordered him to do so. Nick had threatened to pull Heather out altogether to make his new boss back down.

Thankfully, Dante hadn't called his bluff, because Nick wasn't so sure he had enough influence on Heather right now to make her agree to let him pull her off the case.

"We'll be right outside if you need anything," one of the agents said.

Nick nodded his thanks and waited until the agents had left before addressing Gonzalez.

"All right, Mr. Gonzalez. You have your audience with Miss Bannon, as requested. If you threaten or insult her in any way, this meeting is over. Understood?"

Gonzalez's honey-brown eyes focused on Nick.

"I'm perfectly aware of your conditions, Agent Morgan," he said, in a thick accent. "And I assure you, I have nothing but Heather's best interests at heart."

Heather suddenly reached for Nick's hand beneath the table. He flicked his gaze up to hers in surprise, but she wasn't looking at him, so he threaded his fingers through hers and gave her a reassuring squeeze.

"The only thing I want to hear from you," Heather said, her voice surprisingly strong, "is where my sister is. I want her to be safe and I want to bring her home."

"We both want the same thing, I assure you. I love Lily very much, and I want nothing more than for her to be safe and as far from Key West as possible."

"If that's the truth, why are you holding my sister hostage?"

"You misunderstand, Miss Bannon. I'm not the one holding your sister hostage."

Heather's eyes widened. She looked at Nick as if for confirmation. He gave her a slight nod. If anything, her face turned even more pale.

"What are you saying?" she asked Gonzalez.

The chains attached to his wrists rattled on top of the table as he tried to reach his right hand across to Heather. When the links pulled him up short, he grunted and clasped his hands together.

"Miss Bannon, allow me to explain. Do you recall when Lily visited you about six months ago and asked you to go to a convention with her?"

"I don't see how that's relevant, Mr. Gonzalez," she replied. "How is my sister? Have you hurt her?"

He shook his head. "I assure you, I've done nothing to harm your sister. As far as I know, she is alive and well."

Heather's breath caught. "As far as you know?"

"Please, let me explain," he said. "The convention? Do you remember?"

"Yes, yes, I remember. It was one of those identical twin things, where they bring twins from all over the world to meet up and make friends. She begged me to go with her and I couldn't take the time off from work, but she was insistent. So I went with her to registration so she could get in—they only let pairs of twins register. But then I went back home. Why are you asking me about the convention?"

"Because that's where I met Lily."

Her brows drew down in obvious confusion. "I don't understand."

"I was one of the attendees."

"But that doesn't make sense. The only people who are attendees are..."

He nodded. "You've figured it out, I see. I'm not Jose Gonzalez, the man holding your sister. I'm Luis Gonzalez, Jose's identical twin brother."

HEATHER FRANTICALLY SHOOK her head, certain she couldn't have heard him right. "You're not Jose Gonzalez?"

"No. I'm not."

She looked to Nick for confirmation.

"We've fingerprinted him," Nick said. "He's definitely not Jose. The DEA never realized Jose had a twin, but that's the only explanation."

"But…you know my sister?" she asked Luis, her voice hesitant.

"Yes. As I said, we met at the conference. Like you, I did not want to go. But my brother wanted to go." His mouth twisted with disdain. "Not because he wished to socialize, but because he wanted to use it as a front for some deal he was planning. Then he met Lily, and they hit it off."

Heather tried to make sense of what he was telling her. "You sound bitter about that."

"I am. We both liked Lily when we met her. But my brother…he takes what he wants. And he wanted her."

Heather studied his facial expressions, his eyes, trying to decide if she believed him. "Are you a drug dealer like your brother, Mr. Gonzalez?"

"No, Miss Bannon, I am not. I am a businessman. My brother's activities grieve me deeply, but no matter what I do I can't seem to dissuade him. However, when I realized what had happened to Lily, I couldn't sit back and ignore it. I had to do something. That's why I'm here."

His thick Spanish accent made it difficult for Heather to understand him. She had to think for a moment about what he'd just said for it to make sense. "Then you know what happened to my sister and where she is?"

"I know she was taken against her will several days ago from your apartment in north Florida. And I know she's with my brother right now— again, being held against her will—in one of his compounds, but I don't know which one. I've been trying to find out. I want Lily away from my brother as much as you do. I don't want her hurt."

Heather rubbed her temple, trying to relieve the dull ache that had started. "If you don't know where she is, why did you want to talk to me? What were you doing at that dock last night?"

"My men have been on the lookout for information to help me find Lily. As soon as I heard she was in that bar, I headed over, hoping she'd somehow gotten away from my brother. But when I got there I found out one of my brother's men was talking to you inside the bar. I knew he was trying to lure you outside to kill you. I figured out which boat was his and waited."

"You were there to…protect me?"

"Yes."

She gave a harsh laugh. "You didn't protect me, Mr. Gonzalez. You destroyed my best chance to find my sister. That man was going to take me to see her."

"Heather," Nick said, "it's possible he may be

telling the truth. We had a team of agents looking into Luis's background last night, proving his identity. Everything is checking out. And what he says about the man who took you to the boat is valid. That man was one of Jose Gonzalez's most trusted men, known for doing his dirty work. It's highly unlikely he would have thought you were really Lily. We believe he knew exactly where Lily was, and that you were her sister, and he was going to take you out into the ocean to kill you."

Heather shivered and wrapped her arms around her waist. "Then I guess I owe you both for saving my life last night." She dropped her face in her hands. "It's hopeless. There's nothing else I can do. All of this was for nothing. No one is going to lead me to my sister."

She straightened and put her hand beneath the table to clasp Nick's hand again. She hated that she was leaning on him right now, after last night, but she needed his strength, his reassurance. He owed her that much, at least, for making love to her then rejecting her. She squared her shoulders.

"What is Jose Gonzalez planning?" she asked Luis. "Is he keeping my sister alive just long enough so he can tell her that he killed me? Is that what he's doing? Or is she even alive at this point?" She thumped her fist on the table. "All these silly fake tattoos were a waste. No one ever believed I was Lily."

"If I may disagree, Miss Bannon," Luis said, "I don't think it's a waste at all. If I didn't know Lily so well, I would have completely fallen for your trick. I believe most people in my brother's employ would think you were Lily as well. The only ones who wouldn't are his bodyguards and the men he trusts the most, men who have been around Lily long enough to be able to tell you two apart."

Heather studied him for a moment. "You're

saying pretending to be Lily can actually work then?"

"In the right circumstances, yes."

"And yet, you were able to tell I wasn't Lily. How could you tell?"

"It's not your looks that give you away. It's how you hold yourself, how you walk. Lily is a bit more, ah, more of a free spirit. She has attitude. You're more like a librarian playing dress-up."

Nick let out a snort of laughter beside her.

She glared at him and he sobered.

"What do you mean by 'right circumstances'?" she asked.

Nick squeezed her hand beneath the table, capturing her attention. "While you and I have been trying to use your likeness to Lily as our angle to find her, Dante's men have been canvassing the Keys and following up on leads. They believe they may be able to determine exactly where Jose is holding her within a few days. The problem is that, even once they figure out where his compound is located, there isn't much they can do through legal channels. Unless someone actually sees Lily and swears out an affidavit that she's being held against her will, we have no justification for a warrant."

"How about the fact that someone tried to kill us, twice? Isn't that enough for a warrant?"

"No. It isn't. We don't have a firm link between what happened and Jose Gonzalez. We don't have anything with which to make a case. That's where the 'right circumstances' come in. Once we determine where Jose is holding Lily, we'll have to do something, cause a diversion, to get Jose to leave the island. Then we'll use Luis and you, pretending to be Jose and Lily, to gain access. We'll go in with enough force to take over and, hopefully, rescue Lily."

"Hopefully?"

"Hostage situations are always tricky. No guarantees. We have a lot of details to work out. You won't be bait again. I won't allow that. And you aren't physically going to the island. If we use you at all, we'll do it through a video hookup, to speak to some of Jose's men. I'm not putting you in harm's way again."

"But—"

He held up a hand to stop her. "I mean it. There is absolutely no circumstance under which I will foolishly allow you to be put in danger again. I won't shut you out. You can stay here and listen or even help us plan. But that's it. Once everything is set, I'm taking you back to the hotel. And tomorrow morning you'll go back to Saint Augustine. You can do the video hookup remotely, without being anywhere near Gonzalez."

Heather glared at him and crossed her arms.

Nick rapped on the table.

The door immediately opened and Tanner leaned in and looked at Nick. "You're ready?"

"Yes. Tell Dante to get everyone in here. It's time to come up with a plan that will end this once and for all."

Chapter Thirteen

Nick shoved the car into Park in front of the hotel.

Heather reached for the door handle, but Nick grabbed her arm.

"Wait in the car. I'll come around and open your door."

"I assure you that's not necessary. I don't need a man to open my door for me."

Nick's mouth hardened into a thin line. Heather could tell he was irritated with her. That was her fault. She'd been sarcastic and argumentative all day. Then again, that was *his* fault for giving her false hopes last night about the two of them, then rejecting her and then insisting she had to go back to Saint Augustine in the morning while the rescue plan went forward without her.

"Good to know," Nick said, his tone short and clipped. "But we aren't on a date and I'm not playing the gentleman. I'm your bodyguard tonight, which means you sit in the car until I come around and get you out."

He didn't wait for her response.

She grabbed her purse, fuming that she had to wait like a child for him to open her door, but she followed his ridiculous order anyway. He scanned the area several times as he made his way around the hood of the car to her side.

His gun was in his right hand, pointing down to the ground as he opened her door.

Seeing that gun squelched Heather's irritation. It reminded her just how serious everything was, and that she was still in danger. Nick was determined to protect her, no matter how she treated him.

Her shoulders slumped. She'd acted like a spoiled brat all day. She resolved to be polite the rest of the short time they had together. The man was going to risk his life for her tomorrow. The least she could do was to treat him with respect.

She got out of the car and Nick shut the door behind her. He waved for her to precede him up the walkway.

She started up the path.

A small pop sounded, followed by a buzzing noise as something flew through the air from the shrubs beside the hotel.

Nick raised his gun.

Too late.

He grunted, his face contorting with pain as his gun dropped out of his hand. He fell onto the pavement, convulsing.

Twin darts stuck out of his thighs, attached to a long, curly wire. He'd been hit with a Taser.

Heather drew a breath to scream, but her throat closed in shock as a slim figure stepped out from behind the shrubs, holding the Taser. Heather would have known that face anywhere. She saw it every morning when she looked in the mirror.

Lily.

THE SPEEDBOAT SLAPPED against the water as it accelerated away from the dock. Heather held on to the railing to her left as she sat on the rear bench seat beside Nick. They were handcuffed together, and Nick's right arm was cuffed to the railing to his right. Her sister sat about six feet in front of them with her back facing them, beside the man driving the boat—the same man who'd dumped Nick into the trunk of Lily's car, and had then forced him and Heather into the boat at gunpoint. The man might be the muscle behind this abduction, but Lily was definitely the one calling all the shots.

As their speed increased, the ride leveled out. The nose of the boat rose out of the water and the boat practically flew out into the ocean. They weren't running with lights on, but it wasn't like they were going to hit anything. There was nothing and no one else out here this late at night. No one to report a suspicious, unlit boat flying across the ocean. No one to call the police and send help.

Heather clutched Nick's hand. "What are we going to do?" she whispered.

His fingers squeezed hers and he leaned down toward her. "We're going to survive. We'll worry about escape later. Do whatever your sister tells you to do. Don't give her a reason to pull the trigger."

Grief welled up inside Heather, nearly choking her. "I'm so sorry. This is my fault. You were right all along. It was too dangerous. I put you in danger by being here. And all along my sister was only pretending to be abducted. She played me. And I don't even know why. But you're going to pay the price. They're going to kill us. They're going to take us out in the middle of the ocean and dump us."

She eyed the dark water passing by them so fast. "There are sharks, lots of sharks, way out here. I read that somewhere."

Nick squeezed her fingers again. "Take a breath, sweetheart. Try to calm down. I don't think they're going to dump us in the ocean. If they wanted us dead they could have shot us in the parking lot. Instead, they went to a lot of trouble getting us in the car, driving us to the dock and getting us in the boat. They have plans for us."

She shivered. "What plans? Why is Lily doing this?"

"I have no idea. We'll have to keep our wits about us and take advantage of any opportunities we get to escape. Just try to stay calm and pay attention to everything. You never know what detail could save our lives. Take slow, deep breaths before you hyperventilate and pass out."

She took slow, deep breaths, but it wasn't helping. Her heart was pounding so hard it hurt to even breathe. Her sweaty palm kept slipping off the railing.

"Lily is blocking my view of the instrument panel," Nick whispered. "Can you see it?"

Heather leaned to the left. "I see some big, digital numbers. Why?"

"I need to know how fast we're going so I can calculate our distance. What numbers do you see?"

She rattled off everything she could see, which wasn't much. Most of the instrument panel was a blur from this distance.

"Good. That second number is the speed. Let me know if it changes." He studied his watch and mumbled something under his breath, as if he was doing calculations. He looked up in the sky.

"What are you doing now?" Heather whispered.

"Figuring out which direction we're going." He leaned down close to her. "Find the Big Dipper. You know what that is?"

"Of course." She looked up and found the collection of stars above them that looked like a cooking ladle. "There it is."

Nick nodded. "If you mentally connect the two stars at the end of the ladle it forms a line that points to the North Star."

"Oh, I see. Cool. So…we're going south."

"More or less. Now look for Orion's Belt." He watched Lily and the driver for a moment. Then he pointed up to the sky. "There, see those three stars?"

It took longer this time, but Heather finally saw what he was pointing at. "Yes. What does that tell us?"

He lowered his hand. "They form a line that's roughly east-west. So we're going—"

"Southwest, right?"

Nick smiled. "Right." He looked at his watch again. "And if we're maintaining a steady speed, we're about thirty miles southwest of the dock where we boarded the boat. Keep an eye on that speed gauge."

Heather leaned to the left. The numbers were the same. "How is this going to help us?"

He let out a deep sigh. "It won't, unless we can get to a phone wherever we're going, and unless Dante can do some detective work back in Key West and figure out which dock we took off from. I didn't see any landmarks when they opened the trunk and pulled us out. But we were only in that trunk for about thirty minutes, so that limits the possibilities." He shrugged. "It's a long shot, but it might help."

Heather tightened her fingers on his. "You're

kind of amazing. If anyone can get us out of this, you can."

He shook his head, his mouth flattening. "I don't know about that. But we're about to put that to the test."

"What do you mean?"

He pointed to a dark shadow on the horizon. "Because it looks like we're about to reach our destination."

The dark shape came closer and closer, revealing itself as an island, perhaps no more than a mile across from one end to the other. Of course, there was no way to know how deep it might be.

Nick's hand tensed beneath Heather's. She looked up at him in question, but he wasn't looking at her. He was staring straight ahead, clenching his jaw, as the boat slowed and gently bumped against the dock.

The driver of the boat turned around and pointed his gun at them.

Lily dangled a small ring of keys in front of

her before tossing them onto the bench between Nick and Heather. "Unlock your hand from the railing and toss me back the keys," she told Nick.

"Lily," Heather said. "Why are you doing this? I was worried sick about you, thinking you were being held against your will. I—"

Lily laughed, cutting her off. "Your concern for me was exactly what I was counting on. That's why I drove up to Saint Augustine in that rattletrap car and acted like I was down on my luck. I wanted you to feel sorry for me and follow me down here to the Keys. But you were too worried about your precious job and your precious clients. I had to change my plan. It worked. I got you down here. But I'll admit that my first attempt to grab you at Skeleton's Misery was a bit pathetic." She laughed. "I've got you now though. And thanks to your DEA boyfriend, I'm about to get everything I've ever wanted, everything I deserve."

"It was you all along? Not Jose Gonzalez who was after me?"

Lily didn't answer. She motioned with her gun at Nick.

He finished unlocking the cuffs from his right hand and let them drop against the railing. He turned to unlock the second set of cuffs that imprisoned his left wrist against Heather's right one, but Lily shook her head.

"Toss me the keys," she said.

He threw them to her. She caught them and shoved them into the pocket of her cutoff shorts.

"Come on." She waved her hand toward the side of the boat. "Get out and go stand on the shore. We'll get out behind you."

"But I don't understand," Heather said. "Why are you—"

Nick squeezed Heather's hand. She obeyed his unspoken warning and didn't say anything else. He helped her step over the side of the boat. The stiffness in his posture as he walked beside her down the dock told her he was just as worried as she was.

Was Lily planning to leave them stranded on a deserted island, to let them die of exposure or starvation? Was she going to shoot them in the back as they stepped off the dock?

Or did she have something far worse planned?

LILY HAD SOMETHING far worse planned.

Nick pulled Heather to a stop when their five-minute trek through the woods brought them into a clearing. Fifty yards ahead stood a concrete block structure, no bigger than a garden shed. A single light beside the open door cast a dim yellow glow across the clearing.

"Keep moving," Lily called out from behind them.

"If we go in there," Nick whispered, in a voice so low Heather almost couldn't hear him, "we're dead."

"What do we do?" she whispered back.

A gunshot boomed behind them.

Heather screamed.

Nick dove to the ground, pulling her with him and covering her body with his. Her right arm was twisted painfully because of the handcuffs, but Nick still managed to block her from any harm.

When Heather looked up, she realized the bullet had hit the dirt just inches from where she'd been standing. Lily stepped toward them, stopping six feet away. She held the gun they'd taken from Nick, pointing it directly at him. The driver of the boat remained silent, but his gun, too, was aimed their way. Heather didn't know which one of them had taken the shot, but from the dark look in her sister's eyes, she wouldn't be surprised if it had been Lily.

Lily's lips curled back in a sneer. "Get up and get into that shed, or the next shot won't be a warning."

"Stall her," Nick whispered. "Keep her talking." He rose, pulling Heather up with him.

"Go on," Lily said, her voice hard.

"You owe me an explanation." Heather tried to sound far braver than she felt. She couldn't seem to move past the fact that her own sister was holding a gun on her. "I did everything for you. I tried to help you. Gave you money, food, clothing. I was there for you, always."

Lily let out a harsh laugh. "You were never there for me. You were the golden one, Daddy's perfect little girl, the one who could do no wrong. You got everything. I got nothing. That ends today. Go on. Get in the shed."

When Heather didn't budge, Lily slowly moved her gun to point squarely at Nick. "I said, move."

Nick pulled Heather with him toward the building.

"When we reach the door," he whispered, "I'm going to smash the light. We're going to run to the left, around the corner of the shed into the trees." He spoke quickly, his words a low rumble in his chest.

They were twenty feet from the shed. Fifteen.

"When we run, stretch your handcuffed arm out behind you and I'll keep mine as far right as I can to keep you directly in front of me. Remember, Heather, I'm the one wearing a Kevlar vest. I don't want you in the line of fire. Do you understand?"

Ten feet.

"Heather?" he whispered, his voice low and urgent.

"I understand," she whispered back.

Five feet.

"Get inside and shut the door behind you," Lily called out. She didn't sound close, like maybe she and the driver had stopped a good distance behind them.

They stepped to the doorway. Suddenly Nick slammed his fist into the carriage light, shattering the glass and plunging everything into darkness.

"No!" Lily screamed behind them.

A shot rang out. Dust flew up from the concrete wall next to Nick's head. He yanked Heather to the left, half lifting her as he positioned himself between her and their pursuers. They slid around the corner of the building. Another shot boomed behind them. A pinging noise echoed through the trees to their left.

"Faster," Nick urged, his whisper a harsh exhalation of breath near Heather's ear.

They entered the woods on a well-worn path. Heather assumed Nick would steer her off the path so they could try to hide, but he didn't, possibly because the foliage was so thick.

"Heather," Lily called out from behind them. "This wasn't the plan. Stop running or I'll shoot!"

"Keep going," Nick said. "Just a few more feet."

At first Heather didn't know what he meant. But suddenly they were out of the woods, running toward a massive structure, a rambling one-story house that seemed to go on forever. Nick must have seen the whitewashed sides of the house reflected in the moonlight, and that's why he'd kept running down that path.

He didn't slow as he urged her forward. They could have gone faster if it weren't for their awkward position with her arm behind her and his held in front of him, but still it seemed they practically flew across the short expanse of dirt that separated the woods from the house.

Footsteps pounded on the path.

Nick urged Heather around the left side of the house.

Another gunshot rang out just as she ran around the corner.

Nick grunted and fell against her, knocking her to the ground.

He was sprawled on top of her, twisting her

arm at an impossible angle. The pain was blinding, as if someone had rammed a fire-hot poker into her right shoulder. She gritted her teeth against the urge to cry out and shoved at Nick to get him to move.

"Nick, Nick, get up. Come on, please." Was he shot? She didn't know. All she knew for sure was that if they didn't get up, right now, they were both going to die.

"Come on." She twisted around, using her left hand to shove at him. Her right hand hung useless at her side. Tears of pain ran down her face as she tried to ignore the fiery agony in her shoulder.

Nick blinked, looking dazed. He gasped for breath, as if air had just rushed into his lungs. He heaved himself to his feet. "I'm okay. Let's go."

He grabbed her shoulders to pull her up and she let out a shriek of pain before she could stop herself.

His eyes widened, but before he could say anything, footsteps pounded from around the corner. Nick turned and kicked the nearest door. It sagged but didn't open. He kicked it again, grunting with the effort. This time the wooden frame burst into splinters and the door crashed open, slamming against the wall.

Heather ran inside before he could grab her shoulder again. She held her right arm with her left hand, trying to immobilize it as much as possible. A hall opened up on their left and right. She started to go right, but Nick steered her to the left again. He pulled her inside the first open door, a bedroom.

He didn't shut the door. Instead, he urged her back against the wall while he stood in front of her, facing her, inches from the open doorway, once again blocking her with his body.

"What—" she started to whisper, but he vigorously shook his head and pressed his right hand against her mouth. The metallic taste of blood on her lips had her blinking in horror. Nick's hand was covered with blood. He must have cut it when he punched the light.

Since he was watching her so closely, she realized he was waiting to make sure she knew to be quiet. She nodded to let him know she understood, and he dropped his hand. Heather wanted to check his injury, but she followed his lead, being as still and quiet as she could. Her lungs ached with the need to draw a deep breath, but instead she focused on breathing slowly so she wouldn't make any noise. She felt so exposed, so vulnerable, waiting for a bullet to come crashing through the wall.

They both stood motionless in the nearly pitch-black room, waiting, listening. It seemed like time crawled, but it was probably only a few seconds before the sound of muted voices reached them. A man's deep voice, followed by a woman's softer, but somehow harder, voice. Lily.

The words they said weren't clear, but they

must have agreed to go the other way, because their footsteps faded off toward the other end of the house.

Nick pulled away from Heather. He motioned for her to follow him this time as he stepped back out of the room into the hallway. He started to turn right, but apparently changed his mind. He tugged her into the bathroom opposite the bedroom. He opened a drawer and felt inside it for a moment, then he opened another drawer. He grabbed something, shoved it into his pocket and glanced out into the hall again before pulling Heather out with him.

Instead of finding another room to hide in, he quickly retraced their steps back to the door he'd ruined and out into the night. They hurried across the side yard and headed into the brush and trees.

Again Nick surprised Heather by stopping a few feet in. He fumbled with something, but Heather couldn't tell what he was doing. Her shoulder was aching so much she was having trouble concentrating. She still couldn't move her right arm, but it was blessedly starting to go numb.

Her own pain reminded her about Nick's injured hand. She wanted to help him, but he seemed to be just fine and there really wasn't anything she could do.

She shuffled anxiously from foot to foot, turning to look back toward the house. She expected Lily or the man with her to come bursting outside at any moment.

She felt a tug on her hand and heard a click.

Her mouth opened in surprise when the handcuffs fell from her wrist. Another twist and the cuffs unclicked from Nick's wrist, too, and dropped to the ground.

In answer to her unspoken question, he held up a curiously bent safety pin. That must have been what he'd gotten from the bathroom.

"Go," he whispered next to her ear, pointing in a diagonal direction off to their left. "I'm right behind you."

Chapter Fourteen

Nick squatted down in front of Heather. He'd pulled her to a stop a few feet from the water's edge, still deep in the cover of the trees and brush. She was sitting on the forest floor, cradling her right arm as she tried to catch her breath.

He gently swept her bangs out of her eyes. The corners of her eyes were tight, and she didn't even seem to realize that every once in a while she let out a low moan. He hated to see her in such pain, and he hated that he'd been the cause of that pain.

"Why aren't we going to the boat?" she pleaded,

sounding on the verge of panic. "We should run down the beach until we get back to the dock."

"We can't go back to the boat. That's where they'll expect us to go. Besides, I saw your sister pocket the keys when we docked." He didn't tell her that he planned to go back to the house to get those keys. It was their only chance. He'd get those keys no matter what.

Even if it meant he had to kill her sister to do it.

Without being handcuffed to Heather, he had more freedom to plan and attack. But right now, there was something more pressing to take care of.

He eased himself to her right side.

"What…what are you doing?" Her voice sounded wary.

"You know what I'm doing. It has to be done." He gently wrapped his fingers around her right forearm and braced his other hand against her rib cage.

She winced and tried to pull away, but he held on tight.

"Let me go," she pleaded. "It will hurt." A whimper escaped between her clenched teeth.

"I know, baby, but if we don't get your shoulder back into the socket, the blood flow might be restricted and you could permanently lose the use of your arm. Plus, it will feel a lot better. After."

"It's not the 'after' that I'm worried about. How many times have you done this?"

"Counting this time?"

"Yes."

He grinned. "Once."

Her eyes widened.

"I've seen it done a couple of times, though."

"Oh, gee, that's reassuring."

He tightened his hold on her arm and began to gently pull it toward him.

"I'm ready." She squeezed her eyes shut. "Just do it."

He laughed but didn't let up the pressure on her arm.

She opened her eyes. "Aren't you going to pop it back in?"

"I'm working on it. If I try to force it, I could break your arm or damage the muscles even worse. Just give it a minute and let me know once you feel it snap back in place." He continued the long, steady pull. "Talk to me. It will help take your mind off the pain."

"Okay." She scrunched her eyes shut. "Uh, why did you make us turn left instead of right when we went into the house? And later, when we ran into the woods. Every time, you turned left."

"Because most people turn right when they're under duress. It's instinctive, probably because most people are right-handed. So I try to go left if I can, to throw off my pursuers."

She opened her eyes. "You make it sound like you run from people on a regular basis."

"It's part of the job. If you're undercover, dealing with dangerous people on their turf, there are times when you're going to have to run."

"Okay, ouch, it hurts." Her breaths came out in choppy pants.

"I'm sorry, honey. Just a little longer." He hoped he was right. It was killing him watching the pain lance across her face. But he had to stretch the muscles out slowly or he'd end up tearing them.

"When you fell…" Heather panted for a moment. "When you fell against me by the house, did you get shot? I mean, you were wearing your vest, and you seem fine, but…" Her voice drifted off and she clenched her jaw.

"Yeah, the bullet knocked the breath out of me. Stunned me for a second. God bless whoever invented Kevlar."

She laughed, then inhaled sharply.

He increased the pressure, and Heather let out a little whimper.

He was about to give up when he felt a slight movement in the muscles of her arm.

"It's in. It's in," she gasped.

He gently lowered her arm and sat back. "Are you sure?" He felt along the top of her shoulder, feeling for a gap.

"I'm sure. It already feels a lot better." She opened her eyes. "Thank you."

Unable to resist the temptation of her lips so close to his, he framed her face with his hands and gave her a gentle kiss. When he pulled back, her eyes were wide and searching.

He dropped his hands. He needed to keep reminding himself that they weren't together anymore, and never could be. Touching her was dangerous in so many ways.

He cleared his throat. "Be careful with that shoulder. Don't lift your arm up too high or back behind you. It could pop right out again."

She let out a little sigh. He wasn't sure if it was because of that kiss, or something else. "I don't understand what's going on. Why would Lily do this? What does she hope to gain?"

He sat down next to her. He was quiet for several seconds as he listened to the sounds in the woods around them. Something small scurried off to their right, some forest creature probably out looking for dinner. A night bird let out a chirp, reassuring him that no humans were close by.

Lily and her helper were probably holed up in the house, figuring out their strategy. He doubted they'd chance trying to find him and Heather until the sun came up, which was still several hours away. Hopefully by then Dante and his men would have figured out that he and Heather were missing, and they'd be canvassing Key West, looking for witnesses. Maybe someone had seen them head out in the boat, and Dante would send in the cavalry.

But Nick wasn't counting on it.

And he hoped to hell that Lily and her minion didn't have infrared goggles.

"INFRARED WHAT?" HEATHER whispered, her voice slurred from lack of sleep.

Nick grinned. He'd hated waking her—not that she seemed fully awake even now as they walked through the woods—but he didn't feel safe staying in one place very long.

"Goggles," he said. "Keep your voice down."

"But you said no one was out here," she whispered, lowering her voice. "And the sun isn't up yet. You said Lily wouldn't come looking for us until sunrise."

Nick held a branch out of her way. "Just keep moving," he said. "And stop talking so much." He squeezed her waist to soften his words.

After Heather had fallen asleep, he'd dozed for about twenty minutes, a power nap, the way he'd trained himself to do whenever he was on a stakeout with a partner. But once he'd thought about the possibility of Lily having infrared equipment, he couldn't get it out of his head.

Lily had access to an incredibly powerful and expensive speedboat. And the house on this island wasn't exactly cheap. The generator alone had to have cost thousands of dollars. Lily obviously had access to the best equipment Jose Gonzalez's money could buy.

Which meant she and the man with her could be out here right now, hunting Heather and him down with all kinds of advantages.

His only choice was to go on the offensive, which meant he was circling back toward the house from another direction. He hadn't told Heather that yet because he didn't want to scare her. He'd decided their best option was to go back in the house and search for a weapon and a phone, assuming the house had a phone. On a small, remote island like this, there was probably at least a satellite phone somewhere. And if this was one of Gonzalez's houses, which Nick was willing to bet it was, the odds were also high there were more guns inside. Drug dealers tended to keep a heavy arsenal wherever they were at all times.

He already knew Heather was good with a gun. Her bullet had found its target with incredible accuracy, even under extreme stress, when she'd shot one of their pursuers in the garage a few days ago. So if he armed both himself and Heather, they might have a chance.

Provided she could shoot her sister if she had to.

Hopefully it wouldn't come to that. With the sun coming up in less than an hour, they couldn't afford to wait for their hunters to find them.

It was time for the hunted to become the hunters.

"STOP RIGHT HERE," Nick whispered.

Heather stopped, and peeked through the

shrubs. The white coquina shell exterior on the house glowed in the predawn gray light filtering through the trees. Birds chirped, lending an eerie normalcy to a situation that was anything but normal. Presumably, inside that house her sister and a stranger were waiting, with guns, to kill her and Nick. A ripping sound had her looking over at Nick in question. He had his shirt off and was undoing the straps that held on his vest.

"Oh, no, not again." Heather held out her hands and shook her head. "You are not giving me your vest again. Last night you got shot. If you weren't wearing your vest you'd have been killed. I mean it. I will not put that on. I'm putting my foot down this time."

A minute later she was wearing the vest and glaring at Nick as he tugged her shirt down over it.

"Glare at me all you want," he said. "It's not going to change my mind."

She put her hands on her hips. "If you get

shot, you'd better hope it kills you. Because if it doesn't, I will."

"Thanks for the warning. Now you need to be really quiet so I can sneak inside and look for some weapons. I don't want you being so noisy the bad guys find us out here."

"Too late for that," a voice said behind them.

Nick and Heather whirled around.

A man stood several feet away, his face hidden in shadows. But there was no mistaking what he was holding and pointing directly at them—a rifle.

Nick shoved Heather behind him as the other man stepped forward.

Heather leaned over so she could see the gunman.

Gonzalez.

The only question was, which one? Jose or Luis?

Did it even matter?

Either way, they were in a world of trouble.

"You're supposed to be in the shed," he said. "I should have known Lily would screw this up. You might as well go on into the house while I straighten this out." He gestured with his rifle. "Move."

"Luis, right?" Nick asked.

Gonzalez nodded.

"You do know Lily has another man inside the house with her?" Nick said, as he turned around. He put his hand at the small of Heather's back, guiding her toward the house, sheltering her with his body as always—even though she was the one with the vest on this time.

She seriously wished she could shake some sense into him.

"If you're trying to make me angry or jealous so I'll make a mistake, Agent Morgan, don't bother. Lily and I planned this down to the last detail. I know who's in the house with her."

The ruined side door was still sagging open and Luis ushered them in through the opening.

"Lily," he called out, as they rounded the corner into the long hallway. He passed through the archway on the other side into the massive living room and waved Nick and Heather over to one of the couches. He kept his rifle trained on them, his hand steady, his eyes never wavering. "Lily," he called out again.

Footsteps sounded in the hallway, echoing on the wooden floor. Lily rounded the corner. Her eyes widened in surprise when she saw Nick and Heather sitting on the couch.

Heather's stomach tightened and she dug her nails into the soft material of the couch cushion to keep from jumping up and going to her sister. She wanted to talk to her, to plead with her, to make her see reason.

But she couldn't very well do that when her sister was holding a pistol.

"Well, well," Lily said. "This is a surprise." She strode forward, her hips swaying beneath the long T-shirt she'd obviously slept in, which barely reached the tops of her thighs. Her hair was mussed and she smoothed her hand over it as she reached Luis.

She smiled seductively and reached up and kissed his cheek.

He wrapped his free arm around her and pulled her close. "Miss me?"

"Always. You were supposed to be here last night. What took you so long?"

He ran his hand up and down her back, never taking his eyes off Nick and Heather. "The DEA didn't trust me. They talked to me for hours and didn't let me go until this morning. I made them think I needed to go set up some logistics to help with their planned assault on Jose's compound."

"Do they know Heather's missing yet?"

"If they did, they wouldn't have let me go. I figure they'll send an agent over there this morning to check on them. Then the search will begin. Far too late." He glanced back toward the hall, then looked at Lily. "Did you take care of our friend?"

Lily plopped down on one of the chairs. "Yep. We won't have to worry about him ever telling any of Jose's men that we double-crossed him. It's all going to go down just like we planned."

Heather shivered, and Nick wrapped his fingers around hers.

"You double-crossed your sister," Nick said to Lily. "You double-crossed the man who helped you kidnap us. And now you plan on double-crossing Jose." He flicked a glance at Luis. "How sure are you that she won't double-cross *you?*"

A flash of unease passed over Luis's face. "Shut up. You don't know anything about her. She loves me. And she wants to make things right. My brother has spent his whole life spilling his evil drugs into this world. And Lily got caught up in that because you," he spat, glaring at Heather, "took everything that belonged to her. You shut her out and didn't try to help her. She did everything for you. She's the one who worked so hard, but you stole everything from her. That stops today. She and I will bring down my brother, stop his evil, something the DEA should have done years ago. We're the good guys here, not you. We're going to end my brother's tyranny and start a new life together."

Heather shook her head. "Is that what Lily told you? That I took everything from her? Lily, is that what you believe? Explain this to me. Because I remember everything totally differently. I worked hard all my life for what little I have. And I tried to include you, but you pushed me away at every turn. Yet every time you came to visit me, I gave you money I couldn't afford to give. And you took it and left and I never saw you again until the next time you needed money."

"You lie," Lily said. "You were the favorite. You were given everything. And when you gave me money it was only right, because you owed me that money, for ruining my life."

"Enough," Luis said. "My brother will be here soon and we need to prepare. Lily, get dressed. We'll put these two in the shed where they should have been in the first place."

Lily narrowed her eyes at him. "It wasn't my fault. Raul was incompetent. He let them escape."

"Well, then, it won't be a problem for us to put them in the shed now, will it, now that incompetent Raul is gone?"

The tone of his voice was mildly sarcastic. Heather tensed, sensing there was trouble between these two. Trouble between two people holding guns didn't bode well for either her or Nick.

Lily whirled around and stomped back down the hall.

Luis sat down across from them, his gun steady. "Lily is a good girl," he said, sounding slightly defensive, as if he needed to make excuses for her. "She's not accustomed to having to use a gun and breaking the law."

Heather snorted. "Right. That's why she was in Saint Augustine with four kilos of cocaine."

He glared at her.

Nick put his hand on top of her thigh, as if to remind her to be careful what she said.

"Lily is a good girl," Luis repeated. "It was… difficult for her to go through with this plan. But she has a good heart and she knows this is the best way. The world will be a better place without my brother. And you—" he nodded at Heather "—you must pay for your sins against her. Your death will be quick. This entire house, and the shed out back, are wired with explosives. All of Jose's houses are wired this way, so he can destroy them if his enemies try to take him. Well, we are going to use that against him today. And as I said, your death, and yours—" he looked at Nick "—will be quick and painless."

"Let Heather go," Nick said. "She never did anything to hurt Lily, or you."

"Neither did you," Heather insisted. "This is crazy. Luis and Lily are both crazy."

Luis's eyes flashed. "I do not have time to argue with you." The whump-whump sound of a helicopter sounded overhead.

"It is time. My brother will be here soon. We must hurry and put you in the shed. Come."

"Why don't you want us here when your brother gets here?" Heather asked. "Are you afraid we'll tell him the truth, that you're double-crossing him?"

Luis's jaw tightened. "It is not a double cross," he said, his accent thicker than usual as he practically spat out the words. "When you fight Satan, it is God's work."

"Is that what you think you're doing?" a voice asked from the doorway. "God's work?"

Jose Gonzalez stood at the opening to the family room, five men standing beside and behind him. One of the men was holding a squirming Lily.

Luis jerked around but the rifle was snatched from his hands by one of Jose's men.

Nick grabbed Heather and pulled her to her feet. He shoved her back into the corner and stood in front of her.

"I have no quarrel with you, Agent Morgan, or Miss Bannon," Jose's smooth, accented voice said. "My quarrel is with the traitor I call family, and the woman I once called my love."

"I still am," Lily insisted. "It was Luis who tried to betray you, not me. I was going to warn you."

"Ah, so that is why, when my men and I arrived by boat and sent the helicopter as a diversion, we found you hiding in the trees with your gun pointed at my helicopter."

"I was…confused. I thought you were Luis."

Luis let out a roar of rage.

"Enough," Jose said.

Heather tried to see around Nick, but he smoothly stepped in front of her and blocked her view.

"Please take my brother and his lover away," Jose said. "I do not wish to see them anymore."

Heather couldn't see what was happening, but she could hear her sister cursing and Luis yelling as they were apparently shuffled out of the house.

"As I said," Jose's cultured voice rang out after the noise died down. "I have no quarrel with either of you. Please, have a seat."

"Have your men put their guns away first," Nick said.

"Fair enough. Put the guns away. There are no enemies here."

Nick pulled Heather to the couch and they sat. Jose sat across from them in his business suit, looking like he was preparing to share a cup of *café con leche* and churros with friends. Two men stood beside him, their pistols in holsters at their waists, their massive arms hanging down at their sides. They would have looked like a couple of palace guards if it weren't for their khaki shorts and T-shirts.

Jose pulled a cell phone out of his pocket and put it on the coffee table in front of Nick. "Agent Morgan, your DEA friends are on their way here with an arsenal at their disposal. Apparently my brother told them that I was holding you hostage. I would appreciate it very much if you would please tell them not to blow up my island and that you are not a prisoner here. Both of you are free to go when your friends arrive. There are no drugs here and I have not broken any laws."

Nick grabbed the phone. "What about Luis and Lily?"

"Luis and Lily will be taken care of. This is a…family matter."

Heather jumped to her feet. "Let my sister go."

Nick stood beside her and grabbed her around the waist. "Let me handle this."

Heather gave him a terse nod. Nick would protect Lily. He wouldn't let something bad happen to her.

"Deliver Luis and Lily into my keeping," Nick said. "They'll both stand trial and will be put away behind bars."

Jose slowly rose to his feet, shaking his head. "I am sorry, Agent Morgan, but that is not how this is going to work. You see, certain events over the past few weeks have put me in a...delicate position. I have been made to look weak."

"You mean because I destroyed your cocaine," Heather spit out.

"Condition number two," Nick said. "Be quiet."

Heather stiffened against him but didn't say anything else. For now.

"I, of course, do not know what you mean,"

Jose said. "I have no cocaine. I do, however, have a family business and rely on my reputation to run that business. My reputation cannot survive having my own brother and lover turn against me and get away with it."

"They won't get away with it," Nick insisted. "They'll go to prison."

"This is not a negotiation, Agent Morgan. I am trusting you to make that phone call. Do not break my trust, for I would not want us to become enemies. I must go now. Your DEA friends will come here and take you and Miss Bannon back to the mainland. But I do not choose to be here when they arrive." He strode across the room. His men followed, but kept a close watch on Nick as they stepped through the archway.

"Wait, wait, you can't leave with my sister." Heather started after them, but Nick grabbed her and held her back.

"Stop it, you little fool," he said. "We're lucky

to be alive. I assure you Jose Gonzalez doesn't give second chances."

"But what about my sister? If he takes her, he's going to kill her."

"Which is why I'm going to stop him, but not by running after him and his armed bodyguards when I have no weapons." He handed the phone to her and rattled off a number. "Call Dante and tell him what's going on. Tell him not to shoot at the house. I don't want us blown up. And stay right behind me."

She hurried after him as he headed down the long hallway. She punched the buttons he'd told her and held the phone to her ear as he led her into a bedroom. She waited for the call to go through. Nick yanked open drawers and rummaged through them. Then he headed into the walk-in closet.

"What are you looking for?" she asked.

"Guns," he called out, his voice muffled.

The phone crackled in Heather's ear and

Dante's voice came on the line. Heather hurriedly interrupted him. "Sir, this is Heather Bannon. I'm with Agent Nick Morgan. We—"

Heather gasped and clutched the phone to her ear. Lily stood in the doorway, holding a pistol. One side of her face was covered in blood. The gun dropped from her fingers and fell to the carpet.

"I'm sorry," Lily gasped. "For everything. I got so screwed up. I never meant to hurt you. I just wanted to scare you." She coughed. Blood dribbled out of her mouth and dripped down her chin. "Help me." Her eyes rolled up in her head.

"Nick!" Heather screamed. She lunged forward and caught her sister as she crumpled to the floor.

Chapter Fifteen

Gunshots erupted outside the house, the rat-a-tat-tat of automatic weapon fire. Heather cradled her sister's unconscious body and scooted farther down into the cast-iron claw-footed tub. Hot tears slid down her face and plopped onto her sister's hair.

Seeing Heather look so devastated was killing Nick inside, but he couldn't worry about her feelings right now. He'd be lucky if he kept her from being killed, because Armageddon was taking place outside the house.

"Why won't she open her eyes?" she blubbered.

Nick squatted down beside the bathtub. Hopefully it would protect both of the women if any shots came through the bathroom wall. It was the best cover he'd been able to find when the shots started outside.

But if the explosives went off, a fancy tub would be worthless. He needed to get them both out of the house.

Heather looked up at him with wide, tear-bright eyes. "She can't die, Nick. She can't die without knowing how much I love her. How sorry I am."

Nick gritted his teeth. "She knows you love her. And you've got nothing to be sorry about. You didn't do anything wrong."

"But—"

"But nothing. Just wait here. I'm going to see if there's a way out without running the gauntlet outside. I'll be right back."

He ran out of the bathroom and into the hall. He'd reluctantly agreed to put his Kevlar vest back on when Heather had insisted. With the cast-iron tub surrounding her, he figured she was as protected as she'd be in a vest. And he wouldn't be doing her any good if he got shot and couldn't come back to help her.

He ducked down under the windows by the front room and hurried to another bathroom at the front of the house, instead of the one at the back where Heather was. The thicker walls of the bathroom would hopefully lend him some protection. He stood in the tub and lifted the blinds to look out the window.

Dante's men were in a firefight. What neither Dante nor Nick knew was exactly who they were fighting—Luis's men or Jose's men. When Heather had called Dante, his men were already landing on the island. A few minutes later, the gunfire started.

Nick peeked out the window and watched the woods. He counted five different gunmen from his vantage point, based on the muzzle flashes.

A pinging noise sounded and he ducked back, cursing at the small hole in the Sheetrock just inches from where he'd been standing. Another bullet pinged through the wall. He dived down onto the floor, using the tub as a shield. Two more bullets shot into the room. Someone must have seen him looking out the window.

Going out the front was suicide. He needed to find another way for Heather and Lily to get out of the house. He grabbed the cell phone Jose had given him earlier and punched Dante's number.

"Dante," a breathless voice answered.

"It's Nick. We're pinned down in here, and if Luis's statements can be trusted, this whole place is wired with explosives. What the hell is going on? I've got gunfire coming through the walls."

"It's not from us. I swear it's like someone's purposely shooting at the house. We're trying to take them out. We've spotted both of the Gonzalez brothers a few times, but they've got a lot of men protecting them. I can only assume their men are either shooting it out with each other or us. Hell, I don't know who's shooting at whom. It's a screwed-up catastrophe out here."

Nick swore again. "Luis must have had more men hiding in the woods when he came in here. He said he wanted to blow up the house. I've got to get the women out of here. What's the situation out back?"

"Not much better than out front. Your best bet might be to hang low and wait it out."

Another bullet pinged through the wall. The ceramic sink shattered, raining dust and needle-like shards all over the room. Nick covered his head, hissing as the shards pricked his skin like a hundred volts of electricity all over his arms.

"We're sitting ducks in here. I'm taking the women out the east side of the house into the woods. We'll head to the water. Can you cover us?"

"I'll reposition some men. We'll do what we can."

"Give me three minutes."

"You got it."

Nick ended the call and shoved the phone back into his pocket. He grabbed one of the towels hanging on a bar above him and raked the ceramic shards from his arms, leaving a bloody trail across his skin.

He tossed the towel down, lunged to his feet and ran into the hallway. He sprinted down the hall back toward the other bathroom. He didn't want to take the women out into that firestorm outside, but if he could get into the cover of trees, they'd have a much better chance than in here. The house was a death trap of bullets and explosives.

He ran down the hallway and whirled around the corner into the other bathroom.

The tub was empty. Heather and Lily were gone.

THE SOUND OF a voice drifted down the hall. Nick crept forward, following the sound. He held Lily's gun at his side, pointing to the floor. It was a man's voice. Luis? Jose? The voice stopped.

Sweat popped out on Nick's forehead and ran down the side of his face. His gut tightened with dread as he crouched down by the last doorway where the sound had come from. This room was on the back of the house. Thankfully no bullets were pinging through these walls, but there was no guarantee there wouldn't be at any time. The rat-a-tat gunfire was still strafing across the yard.

He raised his gun and swung around the doorway.

Oh, God. No.

For a moment, time stood still as his mind tried to take in the bloody scene.

Luis Gonzalez sat slumped against the far wall. The only way Nick knew it was Luis was because he wasn't wearing a suit as Jose had been earlier. His face and chest were covered in blood. Arterial spray covered the ceiling and walls, and blood was still gurgling from the gaping wound in his jugular. The knife Luis had apparently used to cut his own throat lay in his lifeless hand beside him.

And on the floor at his feet lay Lily and Heather. At first, Nick wasn't even sure which one was which. They were naked, side by side, their eyes closed. It was as if Luis had undressed them and posed them as his last act of vengeance, so no one would be able to tell the two apart.

And they were both covered in blood.

Nick shoved his gun in his holster and ran to the two women. He felt for a pulse. Both of them were still alive, but unconscious.

To the casual eye, the women were identical, especially with their matching tattoos. But Nick knew every inch of Heather's body. He knew the tiny little round scar on her forehead from when she'd had chicken pox as a child and had scratched herself. He recognized the smattering of freckles on her shoulders from when she'd suffered a serious sunburn a few years ago.

Perhaps the most telling of all were her no-nonsense fingernails, clipped short so they wouldn't get in her way—unlike Lily's nails, which were long and perfectly manicured, painted a hot pink.

He sank down next to Heather and gently felt along her body, searching for injuries. When he felt the back of her head, he found a large bump, and his hand came away bloody. He sucked in a sharp breath.

A whisper of sound came from the hallway. Nick grabbed his gun and pointed it at the opening just as Jose Gonzalez stepped into view.

Jose held his arms in the air. His gaze swept the room, his skin turning a pale gray beneath his tan. He stared at his brother a moment. Then he looked above him. If possible, his skin turned even whiter.

"Grab your woman and get out of here," he said. "Luis started the countdown. The house is going to blow." He pointed to the far wall.

Nick looked up. He swore when he saw the square box on the wall that resembled a security system keypad. But the bright lights on the read-out showed numbers that were counting down.

They had less than a minute.

"Grab Lily. She's still alive." Nick shoved his gun in his holster and lifted Heather into his arms. "We'll make a run for it. My men out front are going to lay down cover fire. We'll go out the door on the east side and run into the woods."

Jose slowly shook his head and lowered himself to the floor. He gathered Lily up in his arms and cradled her against him. "No. You go. I'll stay here with my brother. And the woman I loved."

"Don't be a fool. I can't carry them both, and I won't have time to come back for her. If you love her, carry her out of here." He glanced at the readout. "Forty-five seconds. Come on. Let's go."

Heather stirred in Nick's arms. She moaned and opened her eyes. She gasped in recognition. "Nick, what are…" She turned her head and let out a scream. She squirmed and struggled in Nick's arms, but he held her tight so she couldn't get down.

"Let me go!" she yelled, her voice breaking on a sob. "Please. I have to help Lily."

"Jose," Nick urged. "Come on. We only have thirty seconds!"

"Thirty seconds?" Heather whispered, confusion in her tone.

Jose laughed bitterly. "This little firefight has brought down my empire. You and I both know I'll never see the light of day if I go to prison. I didn't mean for any of this to happen, but it did. Luis turned some of my own men against me. I'm finished whether I go to prison or not. At least this way, I'll be with the woman I love. Now go. Get out of here. You may have already waited too late."

Nick looked at the numbers counting down and cursed viciously. He whirled around and ran out the door, up the hallway.

Heather twisted and flailed in his arms. "No, no, don't leave my sister. Nick, oh, God, please don't leave her there!"

The devastation and panic in her voice were like shards of glass to his soul. He steeled himself against her heartbreaking pleas and ran outside.

"Let me go, put me down. I have to help her!"

Nick ran across the side yard. Gunshots continued to ring out, but Dante must have provided the cover he'd promised because none of the bullets hit him or Heather. He clasped her hard against him to quell her struggles so he wouldn't fall while he ran into the woods.

Once on the path, he tossed her on his shoulder, steeling himself against her tearful sobs and pleading to go back for her sister.

He grabbed his cell phone and punched Dante's number, running as fast as his legs could carry him through the thick brush.

When Dante's voice came on the line, Nick yelled into the receiver. "Get your men back from the house, now. It's going to blow!"

He dropped the phone and clutched Heather against him, running faster, faster. The sparkle of blue-green water beckoned in a break in the trees. He yanked Heather back down off his shoulder, clasped her to his chest and jumped into the water.

The world exploded in a fiery ball around them.

Chapter Sixteen

He shouldn't have come to Lily's funeral. Nick knew Heather didn't want him there. She'd made her feelings, or lack of them, perfectly clear by ignoring his requests to see her when they were both in the hospital.

But he couldn't stay away. Part of it, a very large part of it, was guilt. Which was why he was standing here, against doctor's orders, beside some oak trees, using one of the trees for support so he could watch Lily Bannon's memorial service taking place fifty yards away.

He acknowledged that part of the reason he was here was to see Heather again. To catch a glimpse of her brown, wavy hair tumbling down the back of her black dress. To mentally caress the curve of her face as she kissed a white rose and placed it on top of her sister's casket.

There were only a handful of people sitting in the dozen or so white chairs set up in front of the gaping hole in the ground. Apparently Lily hadn't had a lot of friends. And the lack of family members was almost embarrassing. He didn't even know if Heather had any family, and that somehow bothered him even more than his guilt.

He'd loved her almost from the first moment he'd met her. And although he knew her personality, the goodness inside her, the work ethic that was as much a part of her as breathing, he didn't know much about her past, what had shaped her into the person she was today.

He hadn't taken the time to learn.

He'd chosen his career over her. And the only time she'd ever asked him for anything—*please save my sister*—he'd failed her, utterly and completely.

The service was over. He hadn't planned on Heather seeing him there. He'd come to pay his respects, to offer a silent prayer, but he'd intended to step back behind the tree so no one would see him when the funeral came to an end. But he'd been too lost in his thoughts to remember to conceal himself.

Now it was too late.

Even from fifty yards away, he could see Heather's shoulders tense when she looked his way. An older woman standing next to her put her hand on Heather's arm, said something to her. Heather shook her head and started walking toward Nick.

He straightened away from the tree, gritting his teeth against the nausea that action caused and the tug of the material of his suit across the still-tender skin on his back. The explosion had singed the hair on his head and blistered the skin from the back of his neck to the back of his calves. Only his feet had escaped without burns because of his shoes. But thankfully Heather hadn't received any burns. She'd had a concussion from when Luis had knocked her unconscious. And she had half drowned by the time Dante's men had fished them both out of the water. But thank God she hadn't been burned.

She came to a stop about three feet away, the same distance someone might give to a stranger, as if they'd never been anything more than that to each other.

Maybe they hadn't. Maybe he was the only one who felt like his heart was being ripped from his chest every time he thought about the explosion, and how close Heather had come to dying. He certainly hadn't realized how much she meant to him, not until she nearly died in his arms.

"What are you doing here?" she asked, her blue eyes flashing, her hands fisted at her sides.

"I came to pay my respects."

She laughed harshly. "Your respects? To the woman you killed?"

He winced.

"Why did you do it?" Heather demanded. "Why didn't you put me down and grab Lily? I could have run out of that house on my own two feet. You could have saved her. But you chose to let her die. Why?"

He felt the blood rush from his face. He stared at her, incredulous, shocked. Was that what she thought? That he chose for Lily to die? He shook his head. "I didn't want her to die. You had a huge bump on your head and had lost a lot of blood. You'd been knocked unconscious—"

"But I came to. I told you to put me down. You chose not to. There was still enough time to save her."

"You were pale, shaking. Your eyes were un-focused. I knew you had a concussion. I couldn't risk you trying to run out on your own. You wouldn't have made it. You couldn't have run fast enough. The only *choice* I made was to save you. I couldn't save you both."

Her skin flushed and she opened and closed her fists several times, as if she were fighting the urge to slap him, or slug him. If it would make her feel better, he'd gladly stand there and let her.

She didn't hit him. Instead, she drew a deep breath. "You saved my life, several times. I know that. And I thank you for that. But…" Her lips compressed into a hard line and she swallowed. The bright shine in her eyes told him how close she was to losing her composure.

It nearly killed him not to reach out and draw her close, cradle her against him. But he wasn't sure he had the strength to take a step, even if she'd wanted him to hold her, which he knew she didn't. The most severe burns, the ones on his right calf, were sending sharp jolts of fire racing across his nerve endings. It took every ounce of strength and stubbornness he had not to sag against the tree for support.

She blinked several times, fighting tears. She finally let out a pent-up breath, back in control. "I'm sure you feel like you did the right thing on that island, and I am glad to be alive. But I could never look at you again without seeing the face of my sister lying there in a drug dealer's arms while you forced me to leave her there to die." Her voice broke on the last word and she drew another shaky breath. "I don't ever want to see you again."

She turned around and marched across the grass, back to the only person still standing by the graveside, the older woman she'd spoken to earlier. The woman put her arm around Heather's shoulders and led her toward the parking lot.

Nick prayed he wouldn't disgrace himself by blacking out while he waited for Heather to get into her car. His legs started shaking violently, but still he fought against the white-hot agony.

He didn't want Heather's sympathy, and he'd be damned if he let her see how weak he'd become.

When her car rounded a curve out of sight, Nick's brother stepped from behind the cluster of oak trees and shoved the wheelchair up behind him. Nick collapsed into the chair, hissing when his back pressed against the hard vinyl.

"Thanks for waiting," Nick said from between clenched teeth.

"I didn't want you to look like any more of a fool than you already do," Rafe said. "You know it was totally stupid coming here. You've probably set your recovery back a couple of weeks. She would have been really impressed with your intelligence if she'd realized you sneaked out of a hospital to go to a funeral where you weren't even wanted in the first place." Rafe pushed the chair across the grass toward their car.

Nick winced with each bump of the wheels. "I didn't come here for her."

"Yeah. Right."

The agony pulsing through Nick's back and legs was making his vision blur. But it was no worse than the pain of knowing that his brother was right. One of the reasons he'd insisted on coming here was that he'd held a small grain of hope that—if he had the courage to speak to her—Heather might be happy to see him. He'd hoped she might find it in her heart somehow to forgive him.

But now he knew that had been just a dream.

HEATHER SAT IN her car at the curb as she'd done every day this week, and the week before, doing nothing but thinking. Thanks to her sister's one selfless act, she had the luxury of sitting and thinking, of doing nothing, because she could afford to.

Lily had purchased a life insurance policy, a rather large one, and she'd made Heather the beneficiary. The generous settlement seemed like Lily's way of paying her sister back for everything she'd taken from her. It had certainly come in handy, because Heather couldn't focus or concentrate on work ever since the disastrous trip to Key West. Her fledgling private investigator business was on hiatus, and she wasn't sure she even wanted to start it up again.

Thanks to Lily, she didn't have to.

The life insurance policy had been paid for in a lump sum. The only way Lily would have been able to do that was with money from one of the Gonzalez brothers. Heather had wrestled with her conscience for weeks before cashing the insurance check. She'd finally decided that since the Gonzalez brothers had helped to destroy her sister's life, the least they could do was to make some kind of restitution, even if it was from the grave.

Heather had done a lot of looking back in the past few weeks, because she couldn't move forward until she understood how she'd gotten here, why everything had gone so horribly wrong. Talking to her relatives had been, well, an enlightening experience. She'd learned things she'd perhaps suspected, but had never been completely sure of. She'd cried over and over in the days since, but the tears had finally dried. She'd finally made her peace with her sister, and herself.

But there was one more person she needed to make peace with.

That's why she was sitting in her car on the curb in front of a house she'd never been in, hungrily watching the front windows, both hoping and fearing for the glimpse of a familiar profile. It had taken several trips and finally an all-out bribe at the DEA office to get Nick's address. But now, she couldn't seem to work up the nerve to even walk to the door.

Just like yesterday.

And the day before.

And the day before that.

She closed her eyes and rested her forehead

against the steering wheel. Why couldn't she work up the nerve to get out of her car?

"What are you doing here?"

She jumped at the sound of the voice beside her. Rafe Morgan was crouching down next to her open window. The frown and tension around his mouth told her he wasn't a bit pleased to see her.

"I'm sorry," she said. "I didn't mean to intrude. I'll leave." She reached for the keys in the ignition.

"The hell you will." He stood and opened the door. "Get out."

"I'm sorry, what?"

"You heard me. Get out or I'll drag you out."

She blinked, and let out a shriek of surprise when he reached in across her and unbuckled her seat belt. He hauled her out of the car and started walking up toward the house with her in tow.

She pulled back, desperately trying to stop

him. "What are you doing? Stop it right now. Let me go."

He ignored her struggles and forced her all the way to the front door before finally letting her go.

Heather yanked her hand back and rubbed her aching shoulder, the one Nick had popped back into the socket. She was still going through therapy, and Rafe's rough treatment had it throbbing.

His face flushed as he glanced at her hand rubbing her shoulder. "I didn't realize I was hurting you. My apologies."

Heather dropped her hand. "It's an old injury. You didn't know."

He gave her a curt nod. "I couldn't let you leave again without talking to Nick."

This time it was her turn to flush. "Again?"

"I come over here every afternoon after work to check on Nick. And every evening about this time you end up sitting out front, trying to gather the courage to knock on the door. Well, I'm tired of waiting for you to develop a backbone. So I'm taking the decision out of your hands." He turned the knob and shoved the door open. "After you." He swept his hand out in front of him.

Heather balked at the threshold. "Wait, what do you mean you come over here to check on him? Is he sick or something?"

"Or something. He's out back where he is every day at this time. I don't mind telling you that I think you treated him like crap, and he doesn't deserve that. I wouldn't let you near him except that I know the idiot will be happy to see you. Mainly because he's a little bit drunk and too stupid to know better."

Heather's stomach sank. "He's…drunk?"

"Only a little. He just got started. You've caught him at a good time. Now go talk to him. I don't care what you're here to say. Just get it over with. Either make up with him or make sure it's a clean break. Get it all out so he can move on with his life." He wrapped his hands around her waist and physically set her in the foyer as if she were a doll.

She was too shocked to do more than blink at him and move her mouth like a fish, but no sounds came out.

Rafe shut the door in her face, leaving her alone in the darkened entranceway.

Heather reached for the doorknob, intending to step right back outside, but the pictures on the wall caught her attention. She slowly lowered her hand. There were dozens of photographs, family pictures, there could be no doubt. She recognized Nick in some of them, laughing or smiling, the Nick she remembered from when they'd first started dating, the charmer who called her darlin' and made her heart melt.

Her breath caught when she saw a rectangular strip of pictures affixed to the expensive wallpaper with a thumbtack, a black and white collection of five pictures of her and Nick, taken in a photo booth at the local fair. She'd forgotten about that day, had assumed she'd lost those pictures somewhere. She never would have expected to find them on the wall in Nick's house.

For the first time since she'd left him standing in the cemetery after saying those horrible things to him, hope flared inside her that he might yet forgive her. It gave her the courage she'd lacked all week, and had her walking through the house toward the sliding glass doors that opened onto the backyard.

She paused with her hand on the door handle. He was standing with his back to her, staring at the creek that ran behind his house.

Leaning on a cane.

Why did he have a cane? She shoved the door open and stepped onto the back deck.

Nick held up a half-empty beer bottle but didn't turn around. "If you're going to lecture me again, brother dearest, at least wait until I'm drunk to do it." He tilted the bottle and took a long drink.

Heather stepped off the deck onto the grass, a flash of anger finally giving her the courage she'd been lacking. She marched across the grass and grabbed the beer bottle out of Nick's hand.

His eyes widened, then narrowed as he tried to swipe the bottle back from her.

She held it out of his reach and tilted it so the liquid ran out onto the grass.

He glared at her. "What do you want? An apology? Well, forget it. I'm fresh out."

"Why are you using a cane?"

His mouth tightened, but he didn't answer.

"Rafe said you've been drinking a lot. Is that because of me?"

He turned and headed back toward the house. It nearly broke Heather's heart to see him leaning so heavily on the cane. She hurried after him.

"Stop, Nick. We need to talk."

He ignored her and climbed the steps to the deck. The grimace on his face told her how much it hurt him to do that. She followed him all the way to the door, but when he didn't turn around, she rushed to stand in front of him, blocking his way.

"Move," he said, bending down as if to intimidate her with his height.

Truth be told, she was intimidated. He had several days' growth of stubble on his face and his hair looked like it hadn't been cut in a month or more. His hazel eyes had darkened with anger and he looked as if he wanted to beat her over the head with his cane.

She swallowed and reminded herself that he didn't hate her. If he did, he wouldn't have kept her pictures in the foyer.

"Now who's the coward?" she accused. "Big, strong Nick Morgan running away from a woman."

He braced himself against the sliding glass door, his frown ominous as he held up his cane for her to see. "Not so big and strong anymore, in case you hadn't noticed."

Sympathy flooded through her, but she knew he wouldn't welcome her pity, so she struggled to keep it from showing. "Is that because of the explosion?"

He gave her a curt nod.

"I didn't know. I'm sorry."

He leaned on the cane again and stared at her for a full minute, as if trying to come to a decision. Finally, he let out a deep sigh. "Most of the burns were second degree. They healed fairly quickly. But some tree sap stuck on my right calf burned clean down to the muscle. I'm on disability until the doctors decide I can go back to work again."

"Oh, Nick. I'm so sorry."

"It's not your fault," he said, his voice losing

some of its anger. "None of it was. It wasn't any-one's fault. It just…happened."

She put the flat of her palm on his chest.

He stiffened, but she didn't move her hand.

"I know that now," she whispered. "I know it wasn't your fault. It wasn't your fault that any of those terrible things happened." She took a step closer and tilted her head back to look him in the eyes. "Lily's death wasn't anyone's fault but her own. I'm so sorry that I ever blamed you. I don't blame you anymore."

He stared down at her, searching her face, her eyes, for the truth. "What are you saying?" His voice was raw, raspy.

"I'm saying that I was…confused, hurting, and I wanted you to hurt, too. Because I'd just lost my sister. I wanted, I needed, someone to blame. So I blamed you. But it wasn't your fault. I know that now. And it wasn't my fault, al-though I believed it was for a long time. There are a lot of people I can blame—myself, Lily, Luis, Jose—but not you."

He reached up and slowly, as if he was afraid she'd reject him and turn away, traced his fingers over the curve of her cheek. "I'd rather you blamed me than yourself," he said, his voice gruff.

"Can we go inside and sit down?" she asked. "Your leg must be hurting, and I need to explain a few things."

He nodded and pulled the door open for her to go inside.

He limped in after her and lowered himself to the couch, grimacing as he did so.

Heather wanted to soothe his pain away, to run her fingers across his battered leg. But this truce, or whatever it was, that they'd just made was tenuous at best. She didn't want to push too hard. Not yet. She sat down in the chair beside the couch, with a foot of space separating the two of them. So close, and yet so very, very far.

"I never told you about my childhood, about growing up with Lily. And I won't bore you with all the details now except to say that it was…rough. From as far back as I can remember, Lily always seemed to resent me. Oh, we had happy times, but they were when we were very young. Our parents died when we were little and we were raised by relatives, shuffled back and forth. It never bothered me. I always seemed to thrive and excel at school. But Lily was just the opposite. It got really bad after she turned fifteen." She rubbed her hands up and down her arms.

"I always felt like it was my fault somehow, like maybe I shouldn't have tried so hard at school. Or maybe I shouldn't have made so many friends. Lily and I grew further and further apart no matter what I did. And then, on our sixteenth birthday, she ran away. I didn't see her again until a couple of years ago—the first time she stopped in to ask me for money."

Nick watched her intently, as if he were eating up every detail of her life.

"The point is, I always felt like I'd let her down somehow, like her failures were my fault. Like I should have done something more to help her. That's why it was so important to me to try to… save her…when I thought she'd been kidnapped. That's why I was willing to give my life for hers. I felt I owed her that."

Nick shook his head. "You didn't owe her anything."

"Oh, I know that now. Because I was just a child, you see. I couldn't have known what was happening."

Nick closed his eyes briefly before looking at her again. "Lily was abused, wasn't she?"

"Yes." She reached out and took his hand in hers. She was relieved when he didn't pull away, but he wasn't really holding her hand, either. He was letting her hold his hand, without responding one way or the other.

Heather swallowed against the lump in her throat. "After Lily's death, I searched out my relatives. I hadn't kept in touch over the years, but I learned that several of them suspected what I'd never realized, that one of my uncles had abused her. He's dead now, so it's not like I can try to pursue any legal action against him. But at least now I know why Lily was so angry and resented me so much."

Nick gently squeezed her hand.

She felt that touch all the way to her heart.

"She resented you because he never...touched you," he whispered.

"Yes. I don't know why he chose her as his victim."

"You can't blame yourself for anything that happened. You were a child."

She pressed her lips together, nodding. "I know. I don't. It's like I'm...at peace now. Now that I know what happened, and why everything went so wrong between Lily and me, I can forgive her. I understand how torn up she was inside, why she longed for someone to really care about her but never felt she could turn to me. I honestly believe she wanted to protect me from the truth, but that she still couldn't move past her resentment that I was the one who escaped, even though she's the one who ran away."

"I'm glad you don't blame yourself," Nick said, looking wary. "But why did you feel you needed to tell me this?"

Her heart broke at the guarded look in his eyes.

"Nick, I love you. I needed you to know why I said all those horrible things, and that I regret every single word. I'm at peace with my past, except for the part where I hurt you. I love you. And I'm here to ask you to forgive me."

"I forgive you," he whispered. "And I love you, too."

Heather let out a breath she hadn't realized she was holding. "Thank you. That means so much to me, to know you forgive me." She let go of his hand and stood. She hurried across the room, desperate to get out of the house before he saw her tears.

"Hey, where the hell are you going?" Nick called out from behind her.

"Home," she called back as she hurried into the foyer.

The front door opened, and Rafe and his wife Darby stood in the opening. They were smiling until they spotted Heather. Rafe's eyebrows rose and his smile faded.

"I thought you two, I mean, I could have sworn that you would have…" His words trailed off and his mouth tightened with disappointment.

"I…ah, need to go home now. Thank you for letting me speak to your brother."

"Don't let her step one foot out that door," Nick growled from behind her.

Heather stepped forward, but Rafe nudged his

wife back behind him and crossed his arms, lounging in the doorway.

"Detective Morgan, I'd appreciate it if you would get out of my way." Heather was trying hard to hold back her tears. She would be mortified if she cried in front of all these people. It was hard enough to leave without having an audience to her humiliation.

"Heather Bannon, turn around and explain what the hell you think you're doing. You can't tell me you love me then walk out the door."

Heather glared at Rafe. "You aren't going to move, are you?"

He slowly shook his head. She could have sworn he was trying not to laugh.

She huffed out a deep breath and turned around. "Fine. Have it your way," she said to Nick. "I didn't want you to see me cry, okay? Well, look your fill. These are tears. I'm a strong woman but sometimes I can't help but cry. There. Satisfied?" She crossed her arms and stared at the floor, gulping in deep breaths.

Nick limped toward her and stopped a few inches away. He gently nudged her chin up. "Why are you crying?"

"Because I love you, you stubborn man."

"Okay, maybe I'm a little slow here, because I've never been in love before. But I don't get the connection."

Heather shoved his hand away from her chin. "Do I really have to spell it out?"

"Um, yeah. You do."

She huffed again and fisted her hands beside her. "You're a DEA agent. My sister was a drug dealer's girlfriend. Heck, let's be honest. She was basically a drug dealer, too. I had felony drug charges against me. Yes, they were dropped, but only because I helped with a case. I know what all of that means. It means we can't be together. So forgive me if it makes me sad, okay? Now can I go?"

"No."

"What do you mean, no?" she practically screamed at him.

He put his arms around her and gently but steadily pulled her against him. "I love you, Heather Bannon. And you love me. I chose my career over you once. That was the biggest mistake of my life. I won't make that mistake twice. And no, you aren't leaving. Ever."

She blinked at him. "Ever?" she whispered.

He leaned down and gently kissed her lips. "Ever," he repeated.

"But…but…your job means so much to you."

He sighed and shook his head. "I have a past, too. A cousin, whose life was destroyed by drugs. When he died, I vowed I'd grow up to be a DEA agent, that I'd help stop drugs from pouring into our streets. I was sixteen. And yes, I still meant that vow. But, honey, I can help people without being a DEA agent. I didn't think it was that simple before, but I've lived the past four weeks, ten days, and—" he looked at his watch "—thirty-two minutes without you. That's the longest I ever want to be without you again. I can find another job. But I'll never find another you."

"What a nice thing to say," Darby's voice sounded from behind Heather.

Nick frowned.

Heather turned around, blushing fire-hot when she saw Darby and Rafe both standing in the doorway. She'd forgotten all about them. Darby's eyes were misty. Rafe was grinning as if he'd planned this reunion all along.

As Heather thought back to when he'd pulled her out of the car earlier, she realized maybe he had.

She grinned back at him.

Nick grabbed her hand and hauled her into the living room, cursing under his breath. For a man walking with a cane, he could move at a pretty fast clip. He practically dragged her toward the opening into the hallway.

"Hey, wait, where are you two going?" Rafe called out. He and Darby ran into the living room behind them.

"I need some privacy to tell Heather that I love her," Nick yelled as he pulled Heather down the hall.

Rafe stepped into the hall behind them. "But you already told her you loved her. We heard you." His voice was thick with laughter.

"Yes, we did," Darby agreed.

"I need to tell her again." Nick opened a door and shoved it, slamming it against the wall.

Heather's face went even hotter when she saw the bed and realized this was Nick's bedroom. She glanced back over her shoulder. Rafe was leaning against the wall, his grin bigger than ever.

Darby stood beside him, her eyes dancing with amusement.

Nick tugged Heather's arm, pulling her into the room. He hooked his cane on the edge of the door and slammed it shut.

Laughter sounded from the hallway.

Nick rolled his eyes and threw the cane on the floor. He pulled Heather into his arms and kissed her soundly on the lips. When he pulled back, he framed her face with his hands. "In case I forget to tell you later, I love you."

"I love you, too. Um, why would you forget to tell me?"

He grinned. "Because I'll be too busy *showing* you."

Heather shoved out of his arms.

Nick didn't like that. His brows lowered and he took a halting step toward her without the aid of his cane, as if to pull her back into his arms.

Heather held up her hand to stop him. "What about condition number one?"

"Condition number one?"

"Yeah, you know. The one that said we're

through, finished. That there is no 'us' anymore. And I'm pretty sure you said there never would be." She crossed her arms.

His face reddened. "I might have been, ah, hasty when I said that. Let's forget all about that."

"Okay. What about condition number two?"

His mouth quirked up. "The one where you do exactly what I tell you to do? At all times?"

"Mmm-hmm."

"I kind of like that one."

She raised a brow.

He grumbled something under his breath. "Okay. We'll forget that condition, too. If we have to."

"We definitely have to. Now for the third condition."

He waved his hand. "That one said you report to me alone, not Rickloff or Waverly. Obviously that doesn't apply anymore."

"I'm proposing a new third condition."

He stopped directly in front of her, close, but not touching. His eyes held a wary look. "What condition?"

She uncrossed her arms. "That you love me, always, no matter what. And that you don't try to impose any stupid conditions again, ever."

He cocked a brow. "You get to set conditions, but I don't?"

"Works for me," she teased.

He grabbed her and swung her up into his arms. "I agree to condition three, but everything else will have to be renegotiated." He limped with her to the bed.

"Wait, I have one more condition," she squeaked.

He dumped her on the bed and followed her down, covering her with his body. "I'm losing my patience. Make it quick."

"I want you to show me your tattoo."

He blinked, then let out a shout of laughter.

Heather clapped her hand over his mouth.

"Hush. Rafe and Darby might hear us. And we still have to renegotiate new conditions."

He grinned and smoothed her hair back from her face. "That's exactly what we're about to do, darlin'. Negotiate." He leaned down and whispered exactly how he would negotiate, exactly how he would wring an agreement out of her to his every demand.

* * * * *

Mills & Boon® Online

Discover more romance at
www.millsandboon.co.uk

- 🌹 **FREE** online reads
- 🌹 **Books** up to one month before shops
- 🌹 **Browse our books** before you buy

...and much more!

For exclusive competitions and instant updates:

 Like us on **facebook.com/millsandboon**

 Follow us on **twitter.com/millsandboon**

 Join us on **community.millsandboon.co.uk**

Visit us Online | Sign up for our FREE eNewsletter at **www.millsandboon.co.uk**

WEB/M&B/RTL5/LP